Small-g City

S. D. Matley

D1025888

WolfSinger Publications   Security, Colorado

Acknowledgements

A book is the product of many hands. Thank you to the folks who read early drafts of *Small-g City* and offered their comments- -Martin McCaw, Kathleen Beck, Rex Rice and Ann Abraham (my big sister who also taught me to read). Thanks to Tom Randall, Customer Service Chief, King County Metro Transit for explaining how ORCA passes work. Biggest thanks of all to Carol Hightshoe, Publisher and Editor of WolfSinger Publications, for selecting *Small-g City* and bringing it into the light.

Dedication

This book is dedicated to Marjorie Jean Abraham, magnificent mother and unflagging supporter of my creative efforts, and to Bruce A. Matley, beloved husband, First Reader and partner in all things.

ϽΛУ ОΝΕ: ΤUΕSϽΛУ

The summer sun rose early in the Pacific Northwest. Veronica squinted into the east as she circled lazily around Columbia Center, dropped from Fifth to Second Avenue and by the penthouse of the Smith Tower, then swooped up several blocks of Fourth to admire the glass splendor of the Seattle Central Library. Seeing the structures in person after studying Seattle and its architectural history (a project that had spanned two decades of her doctoral century) filled her with the thrill of discovery. Finally she was ready to carry out her case study demonstration, the last step to completing her PhD. The only step she'd omitted in her exhaustive planning process was getting written authorization from Dean Phineas to conduct field work. This was a rare exception in her work ethic, but being on location was critical to proving her case, and she was reasonably certain he wouldn't furnish her with permission to travel, for political reasons. Had he or anyone else realized she was half a world away from campus?

Gritty, humid heat rose stories above the city streets, coating her face with urban brine. Seattle's August was unusually warm this year, she'd looked it up in the Hall of Weather before stealing away from Athens U last night. Her gray pinstriped midi-toga, one she used to wear in her undergraduate days at Athens U School of Business Administration, wasn't ideal flying wear but she was traveling light and the outfit was necessary to her disguise.

Veronica referred to a small, flat screen banded to her wrist. Tuesday 6:12 AM. Hermes, her capable half-sibling employed by the family business, had given her this mechanism—a combination watch, word processer, GPS and communications device—for Beta testing. Wouldn't he be surprised to know she was giving it an international trial!

The streets of downtown Seattle were nearly vacant, the hour early for mortals to report to work. Along Third Avenue a few Metro buses pulled to the curb to disgorge a handful of commuters. She noted the towering Parthenon Building on Third and Madison and nodded to herself, acknowledging she'd return there shortly to begin some crucial undercover work. The sparkle of a stainless steel espresso cart across Third from the Parthenon Building caught her bleary eyes. Veronica's mouth watered at the thought of a double skinny mocha with cinnamon sprinkled on top. She swooped low to check the stand, lower than was safe in terms of avoiding detection as her cloaking was faded from the exhaustion of the long flight. Alas, no chocolate-spiked steam rose from the cart, just a striped awning lifting into place. Disappointed and feeling pangs of caffeine withdrawal, Veronica pulled up and continued on her course, zooming by thirtieth, fortieth and fiftieth story windows of office buildings that still slumbered.

David Bernstein's high-top soles squeaked on the stress mat as he ascended to the number six cart of Use Your Bean Espresso. As he raised the supporting arms of the awning, the red and white striped overhang that smelled like an old tent when the early afternoon sun beat through it, the sky darkened for a second and a chill zipped down David's spine. He snapped the metal arms into the locked position and peered out from underneath the awning at the white-blue August sky and the uninterrupted blocks of office towers that lined Third Avenue. Headed north, a dark figure flew. David couldn't make out wings but his long vision wasn't anything to brag about. Benjamin, a friend he'd made from that one dismal quarter at the University of Washington, was a big UFO freak but David wasn't a believer.

He took a last squint at whatever it was. It had to be an eagle or something big like that. And even if it wasn't, downtown Seattle still needed espresso, even if the temperature was climbing towards seventy at 6:14 AM.

~ ✳ ~

Veronica soared over Seattle Center. The Space Needle slumbered, elevators at rest, tall frame rising above the other nearby buildings, spike pointing heavenward. Clifford, the immortal giant whose dispersed molecules held up the structure, snored like a babe. His lip molecules—beyond detection by mortal eyes but visible to Veronica—fluttered below the roofline. Given his schedule Clifford could sleep later than most, a rarity for a structureling small-g god in this city. Preparatory research assured her that Ralph, the next structureling on her fly by, would be wide awake. Hearing inside her head

Dad's tales about the importance of maintaining secrecy when doing field work, Veronica wearily re-activated her standard-level invisibility cloak, which had faded so badly she could see her own arms extended before her. Masked from mortal and small-g eyes, she turned south, toward the Seattle waterfront. The route was short. She flew at a leisurely velocity and wondered if anyone from Athens U had missed her yet. Her clandestine escape was the first time she'd used her Biggest of Big-Gs-level cloaking. Veronica wondered how Dad would feel if he knew his top-secret proprietary information was being used to deceive him by his Olympus, Inc., heir apparent. She longed for the day when cloaking wasn't a necessary evil amongst immortals, for a new era when the family business could operate with transparency and openness.

She hovered above the upper deck of the raised highway known as the Alaskan Way Viaduct, a pothole-riddled concrete structure considered by many to be the worst architectural eyesore in the city and a prime candidate for collapse in the next major earthquake. Veronica tingled with a rush of adrenaline. At last she was on site with the focal point of her demonstration! Finally she was in a position to complete her PhD and, in turn, revolutionize the Structureling Department, the biggest headache of Olympus, Incorporated. Once the anticipated results were achieved, Dad could no longer ignore her readiness to succeed him as CEO!

Veronica listened intently to the groans that issued from the Alaskan Way Viaduct, groans in a frequency that only an immortal could hear. Ralph's eye molecules, dispersed as all his molecules were to reinforce the structure, formed a broad, faint etching of his real eyes. She noted his eyes were half-closed, presumably with pain, as cars, busses and freight trucks bounced down the north-bound lanes of the highway. Ralph groaned a string of expletives when a cement truck thundered over a metal plate, a temporary bolted-down repair.

Her cloaked lips smiled. The benefits of the new structureling technology should make Ralph an enthusiastic participant in her demonstration. Reassured by the promise of good things to come, Veronica laughed softly to herself. This small-g city would be everything she'd hoped for, as soon as she could get some caffeine to ease the dull headache that had just begun to throb in her forehead. Once fortified, she'd be ready to pursue one last piece of research, something her considerable skill as a hacker couldn't uncover. At last there was a practical application for the theatrical training Mom had insisted she receive as a youngster. If her deception succeeded she'd gain a piece of insurance—a bargaining tool if her demonstration plans met resistance.

The balance of her morning thus planned, Veronica indulged in a loop-the-loop and flew east, toward the spot on Third Avenue where the espresso cart she'd spied earlier would now be open for business.

~ ✳ ~

David wiped down the stainless steel counter and slid open the customer window. His stomach made a noise like a *Drano* commercial. It was going to be a long week between now and payday on Friday. Last night he'd eaten cereal for dinner, saving his four boxes of macaroni and cheese for later.

The mac and cheese was an off brand he and his absent roommate, Mike, had dubbed "Danger Boy," reasoning "You're in danger, boy!" when you had to resort to such food-stuffs. He thought he'd be able to make it through the summer without Mike, who'd gone back to his home town to work graveyard shift at a paper mill, but David hadn't found a summer roommate. Paying the full rent on their two bedroom apartment in the U-District had drained his meager savings account. He'd hoped his boss would come through with a raise, especially when the boss had said David's cart was the top selling Use Your Bean espresso location for three months running. But his hourly wage sat stubbornly at fifty cents above minimum, not much more than when he'd started a year and a half ago. At least he still had a cell phone. Mom had paid his contract a year in advance for his last birthday, which made sense because she was pretty much the only one who called.

David turned the key of the cash register. With a series of electronic grumblings it groaned awake. Third Avenue was quiet, but David knew from experience the morning crowd would appear sometime during the next half-hour. He switched on an old battery-powered radio he'd bought at a second-hand store before his personal finances had turned completely grim and listened to the AM station that played traffic news every ten minutes. *Good business practice*, he heard Dad's tight-lipped voice say inside his head. Traffic information was worth knowing. Backups on Highway 520 and snarls on I-5 could make rush hour brutal for the lawyers, accountants, bankers and librarians bound for the downtown business district, not to mention those poor souls thundering down the Alaskan Way Viaduct.

David stepped down from the cart and trotted to the corner of Third and Madison to take a quick look at the Viaduct, traffic lanes atop concrete piers that everyone worried would tumble in the next big earthquake. A blurred stream of vehicles confirmed that traffic was heavy and moving fast. When he returned to the cart the radio was blaring. A jabber-mouthed traffic reporter shouted I-5 was moving along, too, though a semi-truck had jackknifed in the middle of the 520 bridge and all lanes were at a standstill.

"It's six twenty-three on another hot summer morning," the announcer fired off with the rapidity of a machine gun. "We've had some calls about a mysterious object in the sky from listeners on Highway Ninety-Nine and I-Five near Seattle Center. UFO or weather balloon? You call the shots at station KA—"

"It's an eagle, nitwit," David muttered as he clicked off the radio, stripped off his wind breaker and prepared for a long, steamy morning at Use Your Bean Espresso.

~ ✳ ~

Ka-chunk, ka-chunk, ka-ka-ka-boom sang the chorus of tires and gross weights bouncing along Ralph's back.

"Ouch-ooch-ouch-gheez-oh-shi…" sang Ralph in response.

It was bad for a Tuesday. Traffic hummed along without one lane-blocking breakdown, without one over-burdened mattress truck losing its load, without the eagerly anticipated weekly car fire (which blistered mightily, but it was worth it if a few thousand commuters took a different route). Traffic jams were one of the few events in his work life that gave Ralph hope—weight he could handle, but the grinding vibration of multiple daily rush hours was getting on his nerves. The mortals had no respect, no appreciation for what he did for them every single minute of every single day since the opening of the Alaskan Way Viaduct.

Ka-chunk, ka-chunk, ka-ka-ka-boom.

And this was the thanks he got!

Millennia ago Zeus, the biggest of all Big-G Gods, had realized mortals were designing and building architectural structures far beyond their engineering capabilities—easy to notice as bridges of ambitious span and buildings of perilous height kept falling down on top of the overly confident fools. Zeus had pieced together some of their early experiments, the so-called Seven Man-Made Wonders of the World, before he'd arrived at the master solution: mortals didn't realize many of their innovative architectural structures, from ancient times well into the twentieth century, were supported by the molecules of an immortal giant dispersed throughout!

Ralph gritted his teeth molecules. The only break in the killing monotony of his morning, and it wasn't necessarily a good thing, was the chill he'd felt a few minutes ago when an unmistakable molecular density passed over his top deck. "Big-G!" he'd thought, resisting the urge to cry out the discovery. He'd felt the impulse to pull together into the shape he'd been born with, but had mastered himself, staying the molecules in their dispersal pattern before more than a slight tremor purred through the piers and concrete slabs. He hadn't been visited by a Big-G since he'd taken this job in 1953! Ralph's heart molecules fluttered. Had Zeus come to move him to a new assignment? Was the Biggest of Big-G Gods bringing the good news himself?

The weight of a shadow had passed before his eye molecules but no one materialized. "Cloaked," he'd thought, heart molecules thudding with the immediate interpretation of secrecy as a bad sign. In one of Ralph's weekly counseling sessions, Jim, the regional structureling counselor, had let it slip that a corporate-wide shakeup was rumored for Olympus, Inc., and Ralph wasn't on the best terms with Zeus. Was the boss spying on him, waiting to hear Ralph complain about his current assignment so he could take disciplinary action?

The structureling's paranoid speculations about the hovering Big-G presence had faded when traffic cranked up three or four notches on the pain scale.

Ka-chunk, ka-chunk, ka-ka-ka-boom.

Ralph reached deep into his structureling tool box. He called up a Buddhist relaxation technique he'd learned millennia ago in a World Religions seminar at Athens Tech, drew a deep breath and slowly exhaled.

Ka-chunk, ka-chunk, ka-ka-ka-boom.

The pain wasn't so bad, really.

Ka-chunk, ka-chunk, ka-ka-ka-boom.

The reward of relaxation is relaxation.

Ka-chunk, ka-chunk, ka-ka-ka-BLAM!! BLAM!! BLAM!!!

"OUCH! SHIT! YOW! OUCH!"

A vast cement truck had hit some metal patch plates at just the right speed and just the right angle to bounce and rattle mercilessly, jarring his brain molecules into a stabbing tension headache. By the time Ralph collected his wits and stopped swearing, the cloaked presence was gone.

Ralph groaned in agony, his back molecules sharp with spasms. The pavement needed resurfacing like nobody's business. The temporary metal strips were as dangerous as the cracks and pot holes they covered.

Ka-chunk, ka-chunk, ka-ka-ka-boom.

Life as a geriatric raised highway sucked.

~ ✳ ~

Candy and Jim Smith walked at a fast clip, their feet smacking in unison from crosswalk to sidewalk to crosswalk to sidewalk down Third Avenue. The white-hot morning sun shimmered on Candy's bright red dress. The tight-bodiced garment with short, flared skirt was a fiery contrast to Jim's plaid shirt and chinos. The apologetic stoop of Jim's posture was the artifact of a furious growth spurt millennia ago. During his freshman century at Athens U he'd shot from an undersized adolescent to an unwieldy six-foot-eight.

Apology was not in Candy's vocabulary, verbal or physical. Though a mere six-foot-two in her red platform sandals, she easily matched Jim's stride. Her naturally curly golden mane streamed behind—until she stopped abruptly on a corner and planted her perfectly manicured hands on her hips. A herd of gold bangle bracelets clinked from forearms to wrists like abandoned hula-hoops.

"So what part of carpooling don't they understand?" she said, casting a withering glance at the "full" sign alongside the underground parking lot entrance down the incline to Second Avenue. "I've given them so many incentives—traffic jams, spiraling fuel prices, parking tickets, tow away zones, commutes longer than the work day—"

"Candy, honey," said Jim, stumbling to a halt over his size eighteen Doc Martens and back-tracking to his wife. "Try to put it out of your mind for now." He placed a broad, pale hand on her sun-bronzed shoulder. "Our walks are supposed to diffuse work-related stress, not aggravate it."

That had been Candy's line of argument a decade ago when Jim had started fretting about the Olympus, Inc., reorganization rumors. She'd demanded he take a brisk walk every morning to clear his mind of worry, also to combat middle-aged paunch that had gained momentum as he'd come to spend more time at his desk. The twentieth century's plethora of compliance and regulatory issues had been bad enough—now Hermes' department was booting them all into the digital age. At age forty-six hundred, Jim struggled to keep up with the technological march but he could feel himself aging under the strain of constant change. Early retirement was almost a millennium away.

Worse yet, Candy had passed him on the stress scale. Aside from her usual quick temper she'd been having what he called "women's problems": skyrocketing PMS coupled with increasing pressure on him to start a family. Jim glanced across the street at their favorite espresso cart, swamped with ten AM coffee breakers. He'd try the distraction approach.

"Maybe if we went over to Use Your Bean and bought one of those triple-chocolate cookies you love so much—"

"They only have those on Friday, you idiot!" Candy shrugged Jim's hand off her shoulder with violence. "What are you staring at?!" she growled at a passing trio of men in three-piece suits who'd made the mistake of looking in her direction. Her steel blue eyes flashed, causing the gawkers to peer down at their wingtips and double their speed. "I'll bet you weasels never dreamed of sharing a ride," she hissed in their wake.

"Maybe it's a marketing issue, Candy. Maybe we didn't name it right—"

"Like heck we didn't! They got 'fast food' without a problem." She tossed her hair and snorted with exasperation. Summer was the worst time of all, slow season for Candy's duties as Rain Goddess, Pacific Northwest Region. Naturally energetic and bored stiff, she tinkered with things that were outside her job description, leaving Jim to walk the dangerous line between husband and supervisor.

"It's all a matter of balance," Jim said. He reached for Candy's hand and waited until she looked him in the eye. "Mortals can only retain so much at one time."

From her deepening scowl, Jim knew he shouldn't say one more word to his wife, even in his role as Supervisor, Pacific Northwest Region. He silently prayed to Heaven and Earth she wouldn't ask him if her dress made her look fat.

Zeus be praised, Candy shook her head and started walking again.

"I am so tired of dealing with bozos, Jim!" She gestured across the street at the Use Your Bean cart, its heavy stainless steel fixtures veiled in steam. "You can't throw a discus in this city without hitting an espresso stand."

"I thought you liked espresso?"

"That is not the point, Jim! Mortals can't handle caffeine like we can, and they can't do anything in moderation! If something's bad for them, they want it all the time! Why don't we just put them out of their misery?" She grabbed Jim's arm and forced him to a halt. "Hey, I have a plan." A wicked gleam sparked her eyes. Jim's throat went dry. "Poseidon is probably itching to whip up a tsunami. We could wipe out Western Washington in a twinkling!"

Outbursts such as this, overheard one time too many by other small-gs and reported to Olympus, Inc., had gotten Jim bounced from the position of Continental Manager of Australia to riding herd on Candy and counseling a handful of structurelings in the greater Seattle area. He set his mouth to an overworked, patient smile and patted her hand.

"Not politically correct," he said, and resumed walking, a little faster this time to challenge her stride. "Zeus wouldn't like it, especially if Immortal Resources got hold of it." Jim made a silent prayer to Heaven and Earth, beseeching them to keep him and Candy below the corporate radar in this little-monitored outpost.

"It's their own mortal fault," Candy said, platforms scraping as she adjusted to Jim's increased speed. "They twist the good stuff around and make it into shit!"

"Language, Candy."

Her expression turned sullen as she silently mouthed his words back at him.

"Home again," Jim said. He eased an arm around Candy's waist and shepherded her toward the entrance of the Parthenon Building, a high-rise crowned by their penthouse. "How about a nice cup of ambrosia and a game of *Stratego*?"

"*Stratego* is such a guy thing." Candy bit her red lip and gave him a look no small-g god could resist. "Can't I even do a little bit of— you know?"

Jim balked for a moment—the mortals were sure to notice one of her tirades in mid-August. But now she was curling a tendril of hair around her finger, steel blue eyes warming...what could it hurt, really? He nodded his consent and retreated under the Parthenon

Building awning.

Candy flashed a broad grin. She swept her hands before her, placing a thirty-second freeze on Third Avenue's bustling, coffee breaking mortals and vehicular traffic, then planted her feet shoulder-width apart and extended her powerful arms toward the sky. Energy surged from the earth through her body, crackling and sparking at her fingertips. She brought her palms together with a mighty clap. The hot sky tore apart and the expanding gap filled with heavy billows of gray. She laughed like a child when sheets of rain drenched her, pasting her dress to her skin. "That'll keep 'em indoors!"

Traffic resumed at a crawl, wiper blades springing to action as pedestrians scuttled for cover.

"Feeling better, dear?" Jim asked as she joined him under the awning in two bounds.

"Like I'm on top of Mount Olympus!" she said, clapping her hands together and bouncing on her platforms. "Now let's get busy and flood the media with public service announcements about carpooling!"

~ ✳ ~

Warm rain pelted the sidewalk and rose in a fine mist, like someone had peppered Third Avenue with buckets of dried ice. Tartzilla (her real name was Candy but David preferred the Japanese B-movie name he'd made up for her) stood under an awning directly across the street, cheering and jumping up and down. He'd have to be dead not to notice how her red dress was plastered against her body, wet fabric sculpting substantial curves. Her laughter rumbled over the pavement and through the sparse traffic, and she kept laughing even when her husband Super Geek (a.k.a. Jim) took her by the arm and led her into the building where they'd told David they lived.

David blinked and wiped the steam from his glasses. His stomach was dead empty. The ten o'clock rush was over and he had time to consider which two of the assorted cellophane-wrapped pastries he'd select for his shift meal. Aiming for calories he steamed himself a cup of cocoa instead of his usual latte, then opened the countertop pastry case and grabbed two ham and cheese croissants. Mom hated it when he ate ham, but she'd hate it even more if he died of starvation.

He unwrapped the first croissant and took a deep bite, his

mouth crammed with protein, fat and carbohydrates. For meal allowance he was also entitled to a cookie. Mary the Cookie Lady from the deli down the street would stop by to replenish the dwindling stock of oatmeal and chocolate chip before the lunch rush. He could almost guarantee Candy would be down for two chocolate chip today, and she'd never missed the delivery of the Friday special, chocolate-chocolate chip cookies half-dipped in white chocolate, known as Double-Darks.

Dizzy with caloric intake, David unwrapped the second croissant and was poised for attack when a voice made him jump.

"Excuse me, please."

It was the tall young woman with dark hair, the one in the gray pinstripe sundress who'd ordered from him earlier, just before the morning rush. She stood head and shoulders above the cookie display, under the red-and-white striped awning and out of the deluge. Though she didn't carry an umbrella, she appeared to be bone-dry.

"Tall double skinny mocha with cinnamon?" David said, smiling. A silent moment passed, in which he was caught by her dark, piercing eyes.

"How kind of you to remember," she said, raising an eyebrow.

He instantly felt ga-ga. Maybe the surging of blood sugar?

"Coming right up," he said in a monotone.

David felt dull, almost as if working in slow motion, as he set up two fresh shots of espresso and lifted a sixteen-ounce paper cup from the top of the stack. Running out of money and food was a relentless series of shocks. Should he swallow his pride and stop by the Food Bank on his way home? He pumped the Use Your Bean standard measure of two pumps of chocolate into the bottom of the cup. Then his hand kind of spazzed and pumped two more. The overage tied his stomach in knots. His boss checked inventory pretty closely; Use Your Bean had a policy of bouncing baristas suspected of employee theft.

He set the cup on the counter and popped open the mini refrigerator, meaning to extract the open carton of fat free milk but ending up with whole milk, which he poured into a small stainless steel pitcher and foamed with the steam wand. By the time the milk was heated the espresso was done. David combined it all in the cup, sprinkled cinnamon on top and, his hand moving as if in a dream, topped the cinnamon with a generous helping of dark chocolate shavings. Violently aware he'd added a dollar's worth of extras, his fingers punched the price of a tall double skinny mocha with cinnamon into the cash register. He snapped a lid on the drink and set it in front of his customer.

"Three seventy-five," he said with a smile that felt goofy on his lips, as if the corners of his mouth were held up by clothes pins.

She handed him a bill and wrapped her hand around the cup, smiling for the first time.

"Out of—" he looked down expecting to see a five or a twenty. Maybe the blue, stubby piece of currency was worth that much in its country of origin, wherever that was, but... "Sorry, I—I need this in American dollars."

"Oops."

The girl sighed, nodded, blinked. Though the air was still, David felt the bill flutter. He looked down at his hand. A longer, thinner, bill sporting the familiar face of Lincoln stared up at him. He started to say, "How did you do that?" at the same time she said, "Is that enough?" Her bronzed cheeks flushed and she lowered her gaze for a moment.

"I should have brought more of your currency when I left home. I studied international exchange rates through the three-hundred level," she added apologetically, "but it wasn't my best subject."

"Just right." He rang up the dollar's worth of extras and dropped a measly quarter into the tip jar. In his periphery, he noticed her taking a sip and rolling it around in her mouth.

"Perfect. Just the way they make them back home," she said before turning away.

"Wait!" he cried. He grabbed his windbreaker and held it out to her. "It's raining."

She swung around, lips pursed, and peered beyond the awning at the downpour.

"Oh. That."

"Do you want to borrow my jacket?"

The girl rolled her eyes heavenward, muttered something that sounded like "tut" and strode from under the vinyl roof into the rain. The rain seemed to split a few inches above her head and sheet to either side, like she was walking under the glass dome that covered Mom's anniversary clock. The precipitation continued its retreat with stunning speed, revealing a white-hot sky.

David blinked and wiped the steam off his glasses again, wondering if months of pulling espresso had built up some kind of weird contact high in his system. He had to get out of this mess somehow, find a different job that he could live on, and fast. He'd lost his internet connection a month ago for failure to pay and his cell phone was primitively basic, not enough features to launch a job search. Maybe someone would leave today's *Seattle Times* on a seat on the bus home? If so, tonight he'd scour the "help wanted" ads for something that paid better without having to spend his last dollar.

~ ✳ ~

The mortals pretended they cared, and they pretended they tried to keep him fit, but Ralph knew the word on the streets—the mayor of Seattle wanted to demolish him and route waterfront traffic through a tunnel. At first the Washington State governor had been on Ralph's side, telling the legislature to not even bother submitting a budget that didn't include a gas tax increase for highway projects, of which the Alaskan Way Viaduct topped the list. No one was going to die because it just flat fell down, not if she could help it. "Not on my watch!" she'd said on television and radio, according to Jim.

But all that had changed. The current plan, which had been approved by the State Department of Transportation, favored the tunnel option, replacing the heart of the Viaduct, the very portion of the structure Ralph supported, with two miles of underground highway.

Every minute of every day Ralph asked himself the same questions. Why did so many mortals have to drive to get where they were going? Why did so many cars have only one person in them? What didn't the turkeys understand about carpooling? Something had to happen to get these jerks off his back! He needed a different assignment, something that wasn't open to the public 24/7. The Eiffel Tower would be perfect. Ralph thought of old Reginald who'd had the job since 1889. He must be ready to retire by now? And then there was Briana. He'd practically be able to see her from the Eiffel Tower, instead of being half a world away.

He'd met Briana at Athens Tech. She was a gorgeous British giantess and they were in the same class. Something very special had happened between them senior year, but he'd been ambitious back then and didn't want to settle down. Right after graduation he'd jumped at the chance to work in China, one of a structureling team supporting a series of defensive walls that later became "The Great." Next was the Colosseum job in Rome. Ralph cherished his time in

Italy but he was ready for a change of scene when the bridge job came up in London, and, not too long after that, Briana ended up working in Big Ben! Ralph expressed his interest in picking up where they'd left off. She'd been cool toward him at first but had started warming up just before he got unceremoniously bounced to Seattle and the worst structureling assignment on earth. Zeus hadn't said much to Ralph on the trip west. He'd said even less when he'd dissipated Ralph's molecules and deployed them into the brand new Alaskan Way Viaduct, facing the grubby uphill view of Madison Street instead of the ever-fascinating waterfront and Elliott Bay. It was years later, during one of Ralph's weekly counseling sessions, when Jim had let slip Zeus also had a romantic interest in Briana.

"Youch!" Ralph bellowed. Sounds of twisting metal and cracking concrete joined the rumble of rush hour traffic, the ferry whistle, the ting-ting of that fool cable car gliding back and forth at the bottom of Ralph's pylons.

Here he stood, a structureling in his prime, assigned to a structure that was in line for demolition. If he was demolished before a Big-G reconstituted him, he was toast, finito, yesterday's exploded radial tires. It was one of the very few ways a structureling class small-g god could die.

Ralph's braces shivered. His depressed state of mind killed any hope the Big-G he'd sensed today was here to free him from his agony. He needed ideas, some plan for how to swing the decision from demolition to renovation, like the bleeding-heart public was always doing for that bastard Cliffie (or Pinhead, as Ralph called him in his private thoughts). All the mortals loved Cliffie, couldn't do enough for him in terms of preservation. A landmark, that's what they called him in their half-baked "Save the Space Needle" campaigns. If he could have, Ralph would have puked.

Candy stood at the sun-whitened penthouse window overlooking Third Avenue, arms crossed, shining red nails digging into her forearms. She glared thirty-seven stories down at steam rising from the pavement.

"Of all the nerve! I set that storm for six hours and it only lasted forty-nine minutes! When I find out who short-circuited this—"

"Honey," Jim said. He lowered his copy of the *Seattle Times* and peered through his Coke bottle lenses at his wife. Candy's eyes snapped back at him, flaming with annoyance. He uncrossed his right leg from his left and sat up straight in a soft leather chair the size of a loveseat, bracing himself for the anticipated outburst. "I don't mean to be presumptuous, Candy, but you know what time of the month—"

"Stuff it!" She turned her back to him and continued her vigil at the window. He shook his head and raised his newspaper shield again, wondering why he hadn't learned in all these centuries to keep quiet when she was like this. His stomach soured when he heard her mutter something about "upstarts" and "when I find out who did this." He had to admit it was a puzzle. Outside of themselves and the structurelings, Jim wasn't aware of any other immortals in Seattle, and the mystery was ruining his digestion.

He tried to stop listening as Candy muttered to herself, tried to read a review of the Seattle Opera's current offering before he had to leave for his weekly counseling session with Mavis. The Tacoma Dome structureling was a chronic complainer and know-it-all, easily his most dreaded client. He'd had to cancel their session last week— just thinking about her ranting and raving had given him a splitting headache. Jim hadn't tried the direct approach with her yet, fearing she'd sand bag on her job at great loss of mortal life, but his patience with her griping had worn perilously thin. The mere thought of Mavis made him want to scream.

The doorbell must have rung a second time when he heard it over the exasperated clumping of Candy's platform sandals. She slouched to peer through the peek hole.

"Huh! What kind of an idiot would wear a gray pinstripe midi-toga?" she sniped. "And how'd she get up here anyway?"

Jim rubbed his chin, trying not to show alarm. An unexpected caller was a breach of security. The forgetfulness charm he'd laid at the ground-floor entrances was adequate to prevent snoopy mortals from all but entering the lobby and going back out again, mind blank of the experience. He set down his paper, joined Candy at the double door and stood to one side, poised to cast a backup amnesia spell. Candy straightened up and glared at him as if he'd asked for this problem. She gripped the brass doorknob and gave it a violent twist.

"Whaddyawant?" she snarled at the stranger in the hall, a young woman, tall by mortal standards though half a head shorter than Candy in platforms.

The woman held her smile and didn't make the slightest flinch.

Gutsy, Jim thought.

"I'm Veronica Zeta. From the Central Office."

Jim squinted, confirming the faint, purple small-g aura that danced above her head, typical of Olympian petty bureaucrats. Agents from the Central Office were only sent out for two reasons—either as technical specialists for field-to-Olympus communications or—

"Audit Department."

Jim felt the blood drain from his face and heard Candy suck the air out of the room.

Veronica Zeta, Auditor, looked from Candy's red face to Jim's white one. "Don't tell me the audit notice didn't transmit? I'd better contact Central for a communications tech." She raised her wrist and started punching a series of buttons on the small screen strapped to it.

Jim's brain spun. His feet felt uneven on the floor. The auditor's story sounded true, but maybe she hadn't sent the notice, meaning to catch him off-guard? Or maybe his computer had been hacked? Far be it from him to mess with software of any kind, Jim barely felt comfortable answering his e-mail. Four thousand–plus years of experience cautioned him to hold his tongue. His doctoral advisor at Athens U (a worldly professor named Mentor) had cautioned him millennia ago to only answer direct questions from auditors, not to volunteer any extra information. That, and always serve good—

"Coffee?" he offered.

"Great," the auditor said.

"Excuse me, I have a migraine," Candy announced, and swaggered to the bedroom.

Jim opened the front door wide and smiled as well as he could while trying to stop his upper lip from trembling. Compared to this, Mavis' weekly session would almost seem pleasant, if he still had time to make it after dealing with this new, hair-raising development.

"Right this way," he said, gesturing Auditor Zeta towards the kitchen at the heart of the penthouse as he wondered, "What did I miss?" He'd always been so careful when he'd filled out their tax returns. What red flag had pointed an auditor from Central in their direction?

~ ✳ ~

Lunch rush, and the commuters were really laying it on. Ralph took a deep breath and braced himself against the onslaught. At least there wasn't an evening Mariners game to exponentially increase the *ka-chunk, ka-chunk, ka-ka-ka-boom.*

Ralph sighed, a movement less perceptible to the idiots on his back than a two-knot breeze. He was sick and tired of feeling sick and tired, and vacation was forty years away! What ever happened to the days when he and Jim talked about things besides how much Ralph's back hurt and how the mad rush of traffic was fraying his nerves to the breaking point? Back in the 1950s and 60s they'd only had to talk business for a few minutes (essentially, how Ralph was holding up under the stress of the job) before discussing current events or local sports or talking about their college days. Ah, those were the good old days, when Athens Tech and Athens U went head-to-head at track and field meets! He even used to talk to Jim about Briana, before his memories of her had started feeling like a dream.

Everything good in Ralph's life had corroded in the salt spray of Puget Sound. Zeus had certainly stuck him good, but Ralph's anger at being the victim of sexual politics was offset by professional guilt. Somebody had to be the big, ugly workhorse in this drive-a-holic city! The Alaskan Way Viaduct would crumble without a small-g inside.

Ralph's eye molecules grew damp. He'd worked himself beyond exhaustion to keep the mortals safe and now they were going to demolish him! Would no one start an "Adopt the Viaduct" campaign?

~ ✳ ~

"Candy? Honey?"

It was just past noon when Jim tapped his knuckles on the bedroom door—again. After a pointed silence he dared to turn the knob and open the door just enough to peer through.

"Candy, I'm coming in now."

Thud pronounced an overstuffed red heart-shaped pillow as it smacked the door, inches from Jim's nose. He reduced the opening to a crack.

"She's gone, Candy. She's not coming back until tomorrow morning."

Like lightening the door swung open, Candy filling the frame.

"She never would have come here in the first place if you'd had a professional do our taxes, you moron! I told you this would happen. How many times have I told you this would happen?"

She stormed past Jim to the kitchen and extracted a half-full box of Dilettante chocolates from a secret hiding place Jim could never find. Candy shoveled four cocoa-dusted truffles past her bright red lips and chewed mightily while she poked at her very slightly rounded tummy.

"I'm so fat!" she said into the box, then slammed the lid closed and shoved the box back into the cupboard. "Do you think I've gained weight?"

Jim committed the fatal error of waiting more than two seconds to reply.

"Yes! Yes!" she barked. "I can tell by the way you're looking at me! Yesterday when I took my measurements my waist was one-quarter inch bigger than target!" Candy poked an index finger violently at her waist. "One-quarter inch bigger than target and I'm getting flabby, too! I swear by the River Styx I'm working out as hard as ever. Harder, even!"

Jim sagged against the kitchen island, bumping his head against the pots and pans hanging above, which elicited a harsh "Hah!" from Candy.

"For crying out loud, honey," he said, rubbing his tender scalp, "can't you take something for this? I know you have something in the medicine cabinet—"

"That's for PMS, you dolt! Not for being fat—fat, fat!" She wrapped her forearms around her midsection and dropped her head to her chest, sniffling.

Jim took a breath and counted to ten.

"You're beautiful, Candy."

"Really?" Her tear-filled eyes blinked up into his.

"Really," he said, daring to slide his arms around her perfectly tidy waist. "And don't worry about the audit, sweetheart, I'm sure it's just routine. We haven't done anything wrong."

At least not on purpose.

Jim tapped a kiss on Candy's forehead, loathe to go back to work but he still had to meet with Mavis, not to mention Seymour who held up the old lanes of the Tacoma Narrows Bridge.

"Gotta go," he said, giving his wife a parting squeeze.

She mumbled something about calories, fiddled with her gold bracelets and turned to the sink to fill the kettle with water, muttering about tea. Jim left the kitchen and headed to the picture window in the living room. By the time he'd activated cloaking at level one (sufficient to hide from mortal view), dissolved the glass with a wave of his hand and soared through the window toward Tacoma, fat raindrops pelted from the sky.

~ ✱ ~

Business had tapered off by 2:20 PM, the renewed deluge discouraging all but the most diligent espresso heads. David had cleaned the equipment, wiped down the counter, taken inventory and balanced his till, but his boss hadn't come by to pick up the money for the bank deposit yet. Probably he was running late because of the rain. David's stomach was grumbling again. He grabbed his cell phone out of his back pocket and called his mom. When her voice messaging activated after six rings, he felt like crying.

David flipped the clamshell closed without leaving a message and tucked it back in his pocket. What was he thinking, anyway, that Mom, all the way from Salt Lake City, was just around the corner, poised to pay him a surprise visit and take him to dinner? He'd have to survive on tonight's allotted box of macaroni and cheese. His only other idea, besides the Food Bank, was scavenging abandoned leftovers from the sticky tables at the Center House, home to dozens of fast-food concessions at Seattle Center. Even the thought of this maneuver fell in the "Way Too Disgusting" zone, a full rung below "Danger Boy" on the ravenous young guy food procurement ladder. Maybe he'd make a second box of macaroni and only eat half of it, saving the rest for tomorrow?

He pulled out his cell phone again to check the time. Three o'clock and still no boss. David had a quarter and a dime in his pocket and two dollars (he hoped) in his checking account. If he could only resist giving his pocket change to the first homeless guy who asked he could still retain the feeling of being better than dead broke. He'd never make the 3:05 PM bus to the U-District, the last off-peak trip until 6 PM. Thank god he'd had a $2.50 monthly pass loaded onto his ORCA card instead of the $2.25 off-peak version so he wouldn't have to spend his last quarter getting home!

~ ✱ ~

Jim flew through the living room window shortly after four o'clock and de-cloaked. His glasses were fogged and his plaid shirt and chinos, saturated with an afternoon of non-stop rain, stuck to his skin. Candy, the author of his drenching discomfort, lounged on the couch, sipping a glass of red wine.

"I just love watching the rain," she purred, "especially through an open window. It's like being in a tropical jungle." She giggled when his soggy loafers squeaked, but given her rare good mood it was a price he readily paid. "I'll get the bottle and another glass," she offered, dancing to the kitchen on bare feet as he trudged to the master bedroom for a change of clothes.

She was still smiling when he returned. A pair of their best red wine glasses and an open bottle of his favorite old vine zinfandel sat on the coffee table. Candy, poised on the edge of the sofa, leaned forward to fill the glasses.

"Cheers!" she chimed, clinking her shimmering red bowl against his and watching him to make sure he took a sip before setting his glass down, for good luck. She sighed and leaned back on a plump, square cushion in the corner of the couch. A magazine crackled behind her, a baby magazine, Jim knew without looking. By the River Styx he hoped she wouldn't bring the subject up today, a day burgeoning with other problems. He didn't want to talk about having a family at all, ever, but it had become a burning issue for Candy who looked thirty-five hundred, tops, but would turn four thousand on Friday. To that point, Jim had coached himself to be reasonable and recognize the simple timeline of the immortal reproduction cycle. The gift he'd chosen for her, which, he suddenly realized, still needed wrapping, was an outward symbol of an agreement he'd made with himself. Now all he had to do was to accept his decision on the inside.

The fresh reminder of the issue urged him to take a mouth-filling gulp of wine. Just as the alcohol started to relax him the rattle of concrete and metal shook the building. Jim grabbed Candy's hand and pulled her to the picture window overlooking Elliott Bay.

"Ralph!" they cried in unison.

"Oh—brother! I just talked him down yesterday!"

Jim dropped Candy's hand, pecked her cheek and dashed to the penthouse door, adhering to his strict rule against drinking and flying. "Structurelings are so darn sensitive," he muttered under his breath. "Back in a flash, Cupcake!" he called over his shoulder. He heard the jingle of Candy's bracelets as she rummaged behind her pillow for the hidden baby magazine. Between work and home life the stress never stopped. But even as Jim wondered how he'd managed to surround himself with so many unstable small-g gods he co-cooned himself in the elevator and mouthed the soothing mantra he'd invented on his flight back from Tacoma: *Everything is ninety-nine percent okey-dokey.*

~ * ~

The Fairmont Olympic wasn't home, and that was good. It was not the cramped apartment Veronica rented in the Athens U doctoral candidate housing unit, nor was it Mom and Dad's palatial condo on Mount Olympus where she was treated like a child. The only part of home she yearned for was Bill Gates, Jr., her beloved cat who was being watched by a neighbor.

Veronica hadn't bothered to stop the rain when Candy (whose job title was "Rain Goddess, Pacific Northwest Region" according to the Olympus, Inc., Immortal Resources files) started the deluge again. The wild, zinging drops had helped her stay awake as she finished the day's work, making a quick tour of the other Pacific Northwest structurelings after the faux-audit meeting with Jim.

She'd spotted Jim through his level one cloaking on her way back from the Tacoma Narrows Bridge (thank Dad mortal engineering had advanced to the point where a structureling wasn't needed to hold up the new lanes, too). Jim had just cleared the roof of the Tacoma Dome. Veronica could hear the structureling Mavis' telekinetic bitching as she flew past, two hundred meters above the wooden roofing. No wonder Jim was stressed! Tomorrow she hoped to have the privacy to scour his confidential client files. With luck she would unearth some sensitive information that would, under threat of exposure, ensure Ralph and Clifford's cooperation with her demonstration plans.

But today's work, aside from reviewing tomorrow's schedule and the demonstration planning document, was done. She could relax in her executive king suite, featuring en suite bath and curtained French doors that divided the bedroom from the sitting room. The color scheme of her nest, white through light earth tones, encouraged serenity.

Her midi-toga, wet through with rain, was drying on a hook on the bathroom door. She now wore a complimentary white terry robe and was focused on Hermes' wrist device, which, thankfully, was water-proof. Veronica smiled, thinking how tickled he'd be to hear how she'd used it as part of her auditor disguise. She selected the word processing app and squinted, trying to read the documents she'd stored on it before escaping from Athens U. As soon as her toga was dry she'd go to the store where she'd purchased the brief-case this morning and find a laptop and whatever cables she needed to download it all. The sales clerk, she was certain, would be happy to see the flash of her Bank of Olympus Platinum card twice in one day.

Veronica's eyelids drooped. She set the alarm app on her wrist device and cuddled on top of the king-sized bed for an hour-long nap. She'd been on the go for the better part of thirty-six hours, engaged in the most important and most difficult project of her life. Today's events and the decades of research leading up to it melted from her consciousness. Veronica dreamed of Bill Gates, Jr., purring at her side, the two of them settled in for a peaceful evening with a good book and a glass of wine.

Jim bounced down the steep incline from Third Avenue to Second Avenue, his fresh shirt rain-drenched by the time he reached the crosswalk. He'd talk to Ralph for a few minutes. All he really wanted was attention and who could blame him? With the past decade's vast increase in commuter traffic Ralph's structureling assignment had become the worst in the Pacific Northwest. Jim realized Ralph's workload was every bit as demanding, stressful and relentless as his own. Who could blame the guy for having a mental melt-down?

Sobered by the rain, Jim strode from Second Avenue to First. When he arrived at the relatively flat plain of Western Avenue and advanced to the street nearest the Alaskan Way Viaduct (which was also named Alaskan Way), he activated his sense-around vision. No mortal life forms registered in a nearby alley. He ducked into the alley and dematerialized. His molecules zoomed to the section of the Viaduct where Ralph's face resided. Jim reconstituted himself into a pigeon the size of a cocker spaniel and perched on the side-rail of the upper deck, thankful as always for a counselor's authorization to shape-shift in the interest of gaining access to structureling clients. He made a futile effort to shake the pounding raindrops from his feathers before he poked his head over the railing.

"Hi, Ralph. Everything okay?" he said, his voice a pinched falsetto as it pushed past the point of his beak. Jim craned his neck farther over the edge and stared into one of two faint ovals, several feet in width that blinked under the surface of the concrete like fish against the glass of an aquarium.

"Uh-h-h-h-h, ouch! Sure Jim, everything's fine," Ralph groaned. "Argh, o-o-h!"

A semi-truck bounced hard over a steel plate and raced along regardless of the ear-splitting *KA-THUNK*.

"Damn, I hate rush hour!" Ralph said. "Starts earlier every day and they're not even slowing down for the rain! Do you know how many vehicles I'm built to take in twenty-four hours?"

Jim waited for Ralph's answer to this rhetorical question.

"Sixty-five thousand! You know how many I get?"

"One hundred and ten thousand," Jim cooed in unison with Ralph's rumble.

"It's not your fault, Ralph," Jim said. "No one in nineteen fifty-three ever imagined traffic would get this heavy. You were state-of-the-art back then."

"They hate me now, Jim, everyone hates me."

"No one hates you, Ralph."

"See that reporter down there in the yellow slicker?" Ralph said. His eye molecules rolled left and down, toward the foot of a supporting pier. "She's saying things to make everyone afraid of me!"

"How could they be afraid of you, Ralph? You're crucial to Seattle's transportation system."

The waterfront-spanning structure trembled with ironic laughter. "Nice try, Jim. If I'm such a big, important guy, then what's with the posters?"

"Posters?" Jim preened, trying to look nonchalant though the question gave him acid reflux. "What posters, Ralph?"

"I know you've seen 'em, Jim."

Jim's talons tensed on the wet concrete.

"Over there in the window, Jim," Ralph persisted. "Check it out."

Jim flapped toward a third-story window across the street and hovered in front of the colorful rendering behind the glass: the Seattle waterfront denuded of the Alaskan Way Viaduct. The poster was titled "The Tunnel Option." In Ralph's place was a lavish pedestrian walkway lined with carefully shaped deciduous trees. Jim tried to release the surge of beak-crimping anxiety, tried to replace it with a façade of calm assurance as he flapped back to his perch.

"Not to worry, Ralph. You know how mortals are in this region.

Whatever they're talking about now, it'll be in committee for years. You've got time, plenty of time. Maybe we can get some historic preservationists interested, or—or maybe it's a tribal lands issue?"

Ralph sniffled.

"Hey, come on big guy! Don't cry Ralph, we'll figure it out."

"I've gotta get out of here, Jim!" Ralph gasped between sobs. "If they knock this heap down, I'm a goner. I'd like to know what that damn Cliffie'd do in my position," he said, switching conversational gears with a growl. "One of these days I'm gonna take a poke at him!"

The concrete in the area of Ralph's lips protruded ever-so-slightly before easing back into place, giving Jim's pigeon stomach a twist. He waited for the tantrum to subside.

"Ralph," he cooed, "remember what we talked about last time, about how violence doesn't solve anything?"

"Oh s-sure, Jim," Ralph wheezed, "you bet. Just try tellin' that to C-Candy."

"Let's leave her out of this, Ralph," said Jim, chafing inwardly at his own domestic struggles. At Athens U they'd warned him and every other small-g studying psychology that therapists are best at treating issues they can't solve in their own lives. Knowing and loathing himself as a classic case, Jim fell back on rationalization.

"Ralph, Candy's summer downpours are on a whole different scale than a Viaduct taking a lunge at a tower." The thought of his bride of two thousand years waiting at home in Zeus-knew-what mood accelerated the need for closure. "Hang in there, big guy. We'll talk more tomorrow, okay?"

Talk. Every day the notion mere talk wasn't enough to help Ralph cope with his occupational problems gained momentum in Jim's weary mind. What good did talk really do, for Ralph, for Mavis, for any of the structurelings who really needed help?

Jim held his bird breath while Ralph, very slightly and very slowly, heaved the piers to either side of his eye molecules and sighed.

"Okay, Jim. I promise I won't do anything crazy. Yet."

Jim nodded, ending the counseling session. He glided to street level, beady bird eyes searching for an unoccupied alley in which to reverse his transformation.

~ ✴ ~

Zeus channel surfed from the depths of his titan-sized Barcalounger. The ale in the tankard on the coffee table had gone flat hours ago and the boar rinds on the platter alongside it were stale. He'd lost his appetite completely since receiving the celestialgram from Athens U, reporting Ronnie was missing. Dean Phineas' image had groveled and wobbled on hands and knees, begging a thousand pardons. Zeus longed to review the retirement section of the small-g employee handbook in search of a gigantic loophole to shove the Dean through. Why did so few of his staff believe him when he said the days of zapping displeasing subordinates into the ozone were no more?

Hera sat in a matching Barcalounger alongside his, knitting a baby sweater for the grandchild their daughter Hebe, the Goddess of Youthful Beauty, had announced was on the way. The way Hebe had fussed about ruining her figure the last time she was pregnant, Zeus was surprised at the announcement. All of his kids were head cases, all of them except Ronnie, the youngest and his last hope for retirement. Until today.

"I can't believe she ran off," Zeus muttered, his eyes on the screen.

"I won't say I told you so," said Hera as needles flashed through pink yarn. Why did she always want girls?

Zeus clicked the remote up, up, up, absorbing scenes of natural disaster and political unrest that blurred by like pages in that mortal invention the flip book. He didn't have time for a family crisis now. His schedule this week was brim-full of meetings with department heads and Accounting was on his back again, hounding him to review and finalize the fiscal year-end closing schedule. Endless mortal unrest, administrative details and red tape were the bane of his existence and this week there was no escape. Irritated and mentally exhausted, all he felt capable of tonight was kicking back in the Barcalounger and downing a few tankards, and now even that outlet was ruined.

"Veronica's a smart girl, Zeus," Hera continued. "She's got ideas of her own about how to run the company, and you've got to start giving her the authority to—"

Zeus flicked a pinkie in Hera's direction.

"Damn you, I've dropped a stitch!" Hera's brow furrowed. For a moment she picked at her knitting in silence. "You've got to start treating her like a CEO instead of a child, Zeus," she continued as the needles resumed their smooth, forward click.

"I'm her father! I'm worried about her!" he shouted, his eyes remaining on the screen.

"She's twenty-six hundred years old, Zeus, she can take care of herself."

Zeus heard Hera's lips purse and her eyes roll. He wondered, not for the first time, when she had become such a frump. She was delighted to be a grandmother, a phase of life he found, frankly, off-putting. Her feelings on the subject were millennia away from how he felt—ready to charge off on an escapade at the young age of six-ty-four hundred. Maybe this weekend he'd call Dionysus and ask where the party was. It seemed like centuries since he'd had time to attend an orgiastic revel. But no, there was no time for rest and re-laxation now that he had to straighten out the mess with Ronnie.

"This isn't the first time she's rebelled," Zeus grumbled. "Less than a century ago she—"

The image of Ralph dominating the big screen silenced Zeus's lecture. A female reporter wearing a yellow hooded slicker hunched in the lower right corner of the picture.

"…and in downtown Seattle, commuters not only reported an unidentified flying object headed east over Third Avenue this morn-ing, but were shaken by what appears to have been a minor earth-quake centered at the Alaskan Way Viaduct, though local seismic activity tracking shows no supporting evidence. We'll keep you in-formed as we receive updates, also on the unseasonal deluge that's drenching the entire Pacific Northwest."

"Ve-ro-ni-ca!" Zeus tossed the remote onto the coffee table and shook his fist at the screen. "She's after Ralph, Hera!" he shouted as the heavens thundered.

"And since when have you given two hoots about Ralph?" Hera said in an irritatingly calm voice. "All you ever cared about was get-ting him away from that British girl in Big Ben you used to pester."

He ignored the remark about Briana. "I should never have told Ronnie he was getting agitated!" he roared. "Damn and blast me for not moving him before now! I've got half a mind to go to Seattle and get him back in line myself!"

"Not this close to fiscal year-end you won't." Hera tutted under her breath. "You know Accounting needs you to finalize their schedule by the end of tomorrow."

"Don't 'tut' me, wife, or I'll—"

"You'll what, divorce me and marry someone else?" She placidly knit another row of the baby sweater. "I'm the last available sister you have, you old fool."

"Don't remind me."

Demeter had been his first wife, until she turned into a basket-case when their daughter, Persephone, was abducted by Hades into the Underworld. Even after it had been arranged for Persephone to be home most of the year, Demeter was impossible to deal with. His other sister, Hestia the career Vestal Virgin, was entirely out of the question. Now that his and Hera's kids were grown, marriage was just one more burden to bear. Why did she think he'd want to make the same mistake again? She didn't even try to please him anymore. When was the last time he'd seen her hair down, instead of in that ridiculous braided coif that reminded him of an extremely unattractive wedding cake?

Zeus sighed mightily. Gone were the days of spontaneous visits to earth to stir the mortal pot whenever he needed some diversion. He shook his snowy mane and sighed, longing for the days when he was young and feckless, disguised as a swan here, as a mortal husband there in the pursuit of l'amour.

The mortals were no fun anymore, either. They'd been stinting in their attention to him and the other Olympian gods ever since the dawn of the half-baked notion that they, themselves, could build mighty structures, palaces instead of hovels. But the fools didn't know a thing about architecture or engineering. He'd had to drop most recreational activities to solve the dangers of man-made buildings before mortal-kind was annihilated by vast blocks of stone crashing down on their silly heads.

Then came the catastrophe when history cut from BC to AD. In the aftermath, the world's pantheons suffered a staggering loss in devotees. Everybody from Odin to Thunderbird panicked. Zeus had somehow emerged as the guy left holding the celestial bag for running Earth's daily business while his peers abandoned him, going underground with their dwindling number of followers. That's when the perks of being a god ended completely. No more heroic Big-G visitations to earth, to be recorded in poetry and song—now his job was all damage control and disaster containment, along with all the paperwork, in quadruplicate. He'd had to recruit a vast tier of small-gs to staff Olympus, Inc., including immortal giants to hold up incompetently built mortal structures and counselors to monitor the giants' mental health in every city in the world! Though Zeus would never admit it, the scope of his responsibilities was more than he could handle. And yet, after millennia of being *the* Olympian, he couldn't bring himself to delegate.

"Damn and blast me."

It was time to enact the corporate shake-up he'd been threatening for decades, but how could he lead a vast organizational overhaul when his head was crammed full of red tape?

Zeus' immortal heart cried for a change of scene (though he wasn't due for vacation for twenty-seven years in accordance with corporate policy). His younger self beckoned to him over the millennia, proposing a brilliant plan. Zeus repressed a conspiratorial smile and feigned a mighty yawn.

He flicked off the television. "Time to turn in."

"Good," said Hera. She set her knitting in a golden basket alongside her recliner and gazed through a window at the early morning Grecian sky. "It's not quite dawn. I'll bring in the stars and be with you in a minute."

She crossed to the television and reached for her bellows on top of the entertainment center cabinet. Before she could pull the handles apart to suck in the constellations, Zeus, with a wave of his hand, encased her in stone for forty-eight hours.

"Enjoy your 'time out,' wife. Keep the home fires burning."

Whistling, he strolled to the bedroom they'd rarely shared in the past several centuries. He jotted a quick note, left it on Hera's vanity table and leapt through the open bedroom window. The weight of office fell from his shoulders as he flew through the cold pre-dawn sky. Zeus relished a few moments of soaring before activating his Biggest of Big-Gs cloaking capability and firing into warp speed. With a good tail wind he'd make Seattle in fifteen minutes, just enough time to transform his gold-trimmed toga into a masterful disguise.

~ ✷ ~

Commuters from Bainbridge Island clogged the sidewalks, slogging through puddles toward the ferry terminal and home. Jim, in pigeon form, flew up an alley off Alaskan Way, looking for a spot to transform. Sensing no signs of mortal life, he lit on the cobblestones near a secluded dumpster. Jim's beak softened into a nose, the starting point in his return from bird to man. A filthy pile of rags next to the dumpster stirred and woke when his transformation was half-complete.

"Aliens!" cried the rag heap. "Aliens, come to kill us all!"

A pair of middle-aged women, shivering in their drenched summer suits, paused and scowled in the alleyway entrance. Jim's left arm, the last bit of him to transform (which was, fortunately, turned away from the women) rippled back into its usual form as he silently chewed himself out for sloppiness. Had stress made him such a lightweight that a couple gulps of wine impaired his ability to detect mortal body-heat? He couldn't sense it yet!

Jim fished a twenty from his wallet and handed it to the rag-heap. "You're seeing things, pal. Here, buy yourself some dinner."

The bum snatched the bill and stuffed it in a breast pocket.

"I'll keep quiet this time, boy-o," the destitute man said. He winked lewdly at the women who pursed their lips and strode off. "You'd better watch that hocus-pocus."

There was something familiar about the man's eyes, a glint of mischief Jim recognized but couldn't identify, and it made him taste bile. He had enough worries, between Mavis' bitching, Candy's volatility and Ralph's lips bulging ever-so-slightly from two dimensions to three. Not to mention the audit. Getting caught mid-transformation felt like the last straw hovering above his over-burdened back.

But Jim wouldn't think about that now—he had to rally himself and keep the bits and pieces of his sanity wrapped in one tidy package. It was after five PM and he still had to write up his notes from today's counseling sessions, plus dig up eight decades of tax records and put a small-g-proof lock on his client filing cabinet.

"Everything is ninety-nine percent okey-dokey," Jim chanted to himself as he scaled Madison Avenue, back to Candy, back to fretting about the audit. And it was only Tuesday.

∂ay two: we∂neS∂ay

Another morning, another day of pulling espresso. David felt unsettled and nutritionally bereft as he raised the striped awning to fend off the promise of another white-hot day, unless there was another unpredicted deluge. Seattle was the weird weather capital of the world, but it sure beat Utah, especially if you were Jewish.

In Salt Lake City he'd left a coddling social worker mother and a highly focused CPA dad who expected him to excel in his freshman and sophomore years, ace the accounting 100 and 200 levels, and top the list of applicants to the University of Washington Foster School of Business Administration. Far from sharing his dad's enthusiasm, David had washed out in the first quarter, when the concept of the present value of an annuity was presented. The concept had missed every brain cell he had and ricocheted off into space where some alien culture could truly appreciate it. The next week David switched Accounting 101 from graded to pass/fail, and at quarter's end explained to Dad that he'd landed on the "fail" end of the grading continuum. That was more than a year and a half ago. They hadn't talked much since, unlike Mom who called every day. He realized with a jolt she hadn't called him yesterday.

David resolved to call her when he had a break. He made a final inspection of his set-up before declaring the cart officially open. As he polished a smudge off the stainless steel counter he noticed the girl with the pinstriped sundress across the street. Kind of weird for a girl to wear the same thing two days in a row, but maybe that was how people dressed wherever she came from? She carried a briefcase and entered the Parthenon Building, the one Tartzilla and Super Geek called home. Would she stop by the cart again today? The prospect chilled him with a mixture of excitement and fear. He'd woken up in the middle of the night in a cold sweat, remembering the stubby blue piece of currency she'd handed him that changed into a five.

But that couldn't be right, must have been a nightmare brought on by last night's dinner. The two boxes of "Danger Boy" macaroni had left him feeling simultaneously blocked up and hollow. His rations were down to one box for tonight, one box for Thursday, with only water to add to the cheese powder for sauce.

And then—Friday! The miracle of the paycheck! His mouth watered for fresh fruit, a glass of milk, a salad, and he didn't even like salad. He hadn't found a discarded "help wanted" section from the *Seattle Times* on the bus home last night, but the prospect of decent food in a couple of days gave him confidence his life would soon change for the better.

~ ✳ ~

Veronica arrived at Jim and Candy's penthouse shortly after dawn, armed with her prop briefcase. She touched the doorbell and waited through a chime-produced snippet she recognized as "Louie Louie," the official Washington State song she'd heard online during her research. Her wrist device counted three digital minutes and seventeen seconds without a stir on the other side of the door. Veronica knocked, briskly. And knocked again. And again.

Finally the door retreated from her throbbing knuckles. Above the chain (which she didn't remember seeing the day before) appeared a stubbly-faced apparition in a rumpled plaid shirt and chinos who uttered, "Mumph?"

She stepped back to avoid a cloud of morning breath. "Veronica Zeta here. Good morning, Jim. Are we ready to start?"

Jim's eyelids lifted from quarter-open to half. "Coffee," he mumbled. He unchained the door and gestured to her to follow him to the kitchen.

Veronica set her briefcase on the black granite kitchen island counter and sat on one of two stools. For a moment she wondered if Jim and Candy felt lonely, stationed in a city where all the other small-gs were dispersed into architectural structures. She punched the word "company" into her wrist device as a reminder to add this benefit of the new technology to her dissertation. Jim, his back to her, busied himself with a home espresso maker more elaborate than the one operated by the boy at the cart across the street.

"You?" Jim said, turning to her, eyes fully open but still bleary.

Yesterday he'd offered drip coffee from a fresh pot, but since he was asking.... She studied the bottles of syrups and other flavorings flanking the espresso machine.

"Tall double skinny mocha with cinnamon."

She didn't dare blow her small-g cover by uncloaking her Big-G golden super-aura, a necessary step to activating her mind-bending powers. Jim poured milk from a carton marked "non-fat" into the frothing pitcher and stirred a mere two shots of chocolate into the espresso. He handed her the weak copy of her favorite beverage and turned back to the espresso machine.

"What are you having?"

"Americano," he said as he set up a triple-shot of espresso.

Veronica wiggled her index finger to fabricate an AUD-SG-Form 2000 (at least what she remembered of the form from her research) from the nearby molecules. The document that materialized in her hand was shiny with a slight copper tinge. She glanced up at the collection of gourmet pans hanging from the pot rack, noting a dull faded spot on the bottom of the nearest pan. Hopefully she wouldn't have to create many more forms while they were in the kitchen.

"We'll start with the preliminary questionnaire," she said. She unsnapped the latches of her briefcase while his back was turned and pretended to extract the form from within.

Jim settled on the stool across from her and sipped from a green and yellow cup sporting the word "Sonics." He nodded toward the AUD-SG-Form 2000 that lay on the counter between them.

"Shiny paper," he remarked.

"It's specially made, to hold up through long-term storage," she fibbed, sipping her mocha.

"Interesting." He picked up the form and rubbed it between thumb and forefinger. "How's your mocha?"

"What?"

He was looking at her like he was trying to decode something, his expression apologetic.

"Your mocha," he repeated, tapping his own mug. "You made a face when you were sipping just now. Has the milk soured?"

"Uh, no, it's fine, perfectly fine."

"Oh!" His eyes brightened. "I'll bet I know what it is! I'll bet you're watching your weight! That's why you wanted it 'skinny' but you're not used to it, right?"

Veronica's face blazed. She sat up as straight as a Doric column. "What?!" Her golden super-aura roiled under the cloaking.

"Oh for Zeus' sake, I can't believe I just said that! I'm so sorry Miss Zeta, I must not be awake yet. But it just struck me that Candy—my wife—when she's trying to watch her weight—and believe me, I've always thought she looks just perfect—well. Uhm."

Veronica rummaged in her briefcase, fabricating a pen from the lining during the embarrassing silence. "Your full name, Jim?" she said, pulling the questionnaire toward her.

"James A. Smith."

"'A' for?"

A few beats passed. "Ares," he said, shrugging his shoulders.

"Ares," she repeated, thinking with distaste of her obnoxious sibling by that name as she filled in the blank.

"Not a name you'd expect for a guy like me, I know, but it was a popular name for boys the century I was born. Don't worry, though," he chattered on, "I'm definitely anti-war. But I do like a well-matched game of *Stratego* every so often."

"Of what?"

"*Stratego*," he repeated. "A mortal game, kind of like Zeus' chess board, only it's made out of cardboard and plastic. And it's pretend."

She noted the unfamiliar word in the "comments" section at the bottom of the form. Dad was hard to buy gifts for and she'd like to give him something besides the usual stack of spy-thriller novels for his next birthday.

"Okay," she said, after recording this unexpectedly useful piece of information. "Occupation?"

"Counselor."

"Title?"

"Regional Supervisor Pacific Northwest Region and Structurel-ing Advisor."

"Rank?"

"S-g seventeen."

"You're a *seventeen?*" She paused and looked at him, seeing the hint of a modest smile. "That's great for someone your age. You can't be much over four thousand."

"Four thousand six-hundred and ninety-three," he said blushing.

"But still," she said, "what's a seventeen doing in a dinky little region like this? I thought you guys automatically rated continents, or at least an entire major country? You should have been promoted decades ago!"

"Oh I was. I was," he said eagerly. "But. Well. We, uh—"

"Where in the River Styx is my conditioner?" roared a voice in the distance.

"We have special needs," Jim finished quickly. He darted out of the kitchen and padded in the direction of the voice. "Left side of the medicine cabinet, Cupcake," he said from a room away. "Let me find it for you," he said from farther still.

Veronica gulped down her alleged tall double skinny mocha with cinnamon. "Special needs. Right." Dad was counting on a henpecked, demoted sg-17 to keep Ralph sane in that beaten-up wreck of a raised highway. At a minimum Jim needed marriage counseling and someone named Zeus was long overdue for retirement.

She shuddered as she listened to the mixture of ranting, tears, pleading and, finally, a heavy-duty shower massage pulsing in a distant corner of the penthouse. For all her strength of character and self-discipline, the one thing that drained Veronica instantly was marital squabbling. Mom and Dad argued a lot, so much and so bitterly she'd come to wonder why anyone would want to get married in the first place. She'd vowed centuries ago not to take on that particular aggravation.

She glanced up at the pot rack and twitched her little finger, observing how dull the pan bottoms grew as she conjured a small copper-tinted notebook and scrawled "gone for coffee" across a blank page, which she tore out and weighted with Jim's mug. She'd will the kid at the espresso stand to make a tall skinny double mocha with cinnamon the right way while the hideous small-g marital dust settled.

Hera fumed inside her stone prison. She'd been trapped there since dawn and deadlines were flying by. She felt like she'd never catch up with the new program they were designing at work, tentatively called "Marriage and the Media." She'd planned to take a two-hour nap instead of sleeping her usual six hours before Zeus had confined her. That would have given her time to finish the outline for the upcoming Prevention of Bad Marriages summit meeting. She'd promised her executive assistant she'd have it ready this afternoon, but at 4 PM Mount Olympus time Hera had more than a day to serve as a captive.

If she could only ball her fists to express her outrage! Every time Zeus did this to her she suffered a tidal wave of humiliation and anger. He was on another spree of so-called "field work." What would he appear as this time, she wondered—a swan, or maybe a bull? And who would be the lucky woman (or animal or tree—whatever) to receive his favors? It made her look damned bad. Hera, the Goddess of Marriage, couldn't keep the old man happy at home.

Not that she was perfect, Hera thought with a grim inner smile. She'd strayed from the conjugal bed exactly once, just to get even, but she'd never got the chance to tell Zeus because it happened just before the switch from BC to AD. When she was poised to confess and extract her vengeance he wouldn't make time to talk. Hera's grim inner smile deepened. What would his Eternal Pomposity think if he heard about the two-millennium-old secret now?

He'd be enraged, of course, would make a terrible fuss about how she'd betrayed him. The stone surrounding Hera vibrated with sour, silent laughter. For himself, Zeus always made excuses. The pressure of work was his stock rationale for cheating or anything else he did that was immature and disgusting. Their sister Demeter, Zeus' first wife, had suffered the same insults, but it hadn't mattered much to her. All she cared about was when their daughter, Persephone, would come home to visit.

"I should be so lucky," Hera thought. Wouldn't it be great if absenteeism was the only thing wrong with her kids? Ronnie was the exception—the other four more or less personified the box of maladies Pandora had unleashed on the world. Frozen in place with nothing but the thoughts that kept her awake at night, Hera ruminated about her wretched children.

Hef (the nickname Hephaestus insisted they all use) was the family hot-head and always had been, ever since he was a little boy playing with fire. As a teenager he'd loved blowing things up. That's when Zeus suggested making him the God of Volcanoes as a coming-of-age present. It had seemed a positive way to direct the boy's energy until he got obsessed with war. They'd intervened and directed him towards the production of arms and armaments instead of actual fighting. A segue to the fine arts was the overall plan—metal sculpting, casting, etc.—and he was doing better now. Just last Monday he'd sent a gorgeous gold necklace in a laurel pattern he'd made himself with a note saying, "Mom, you're my hero," but he still liked to blow things up.

Hebe was a minor but important goddess, as the therapist had reminded her in weekly sessions during her difficult sixteenth century. At that time her official title, Goddess of Youthful Beauty, generally sent her out of the room in tears. This behavior crested with an episode of door slamming and pouting when Hef had teased her about a pimple the night of her debut. Hera could hear the wailing and crying even now. "You think it's easy, you big jerk! How would you like it if your only selling point was your ugly mug?!" Fortunately Hebe had made a good marriage, and she and Heracles had two children. But they'd also designated Hera as unpaid babysitter, even though grandma worked full time!

Ilithyia—it had seemed a good name at first, but they'd shortened it to Elle—was the Goddess of Childbirth and Midwifery. She'd become a radical feminist after being called upon century after century to relieve the pain of childbirth. Who could blame her? Every so often Hera saw Elle surf by on Zeus' big screen TV, leading a march for Zero Population Growth. The girl looked awful. She'd traded her toga for the wretched mortal uniform of jeans and a tee shirt, and her ultra-short punk hairstyle over-emphasized the narrowness of her face. It made her look like a weasel. Seeing Elle made Hera want to kidnap her and give her a make-over.

And then there was Ares. Zeus had tried to duck all responsibility for this one (at two centuries old he was tormenting the household pets) by claiming Hera had somehow managed to get herself pregnant with a magical flower! Ares was a bully and a coward. Naturally he'd jumped at the opportunity to be God of War when Hef was redirected to the fine arts. When Hef had been in charge, wars were still about things that mattered—villages stealing cattle from each other or rebellion against a tyrant. But once Ares got his hands on the division he encouraged wars over mere thoughts and ideas! Just thinking about it gave Hera an Olympus-sized headache. Ares was always running out of funds and dogging Zeus for additional appropriations. Hera prayed to Heaven and Earth Ares wouldn't show up while she was trapped in stone. He'd certainly take advantage of the situation and raid the mad money she kept in an old Cretan vase in the pantry.

As for Zeus' other children—well! She'd given up counting how many he'd fathered in the name of "field work." The family business was layers deep in gods and demi-gods of all descriptions, not to mention all the nieces and nephews, courtesy of Poseidon and Hades. Fortunately, Demeter's Persephone had married Hades and had a real job in the Underworld, and their sister Hestia's career precluded her from having a family. The worst thing Zeus had ever done to Hera was assigning her the official task of organizing family celebrations. She had one full-time assistant dedicated to keeping up with the hassle of buying and sending cards and presents alone. Zeus, naturally, couldn't be bothered with such trifles. "They're your nieces and nephews," he'd say about the children he'd spawned out-side of marriage, as if this absolved him from responsibility!

Hera's teeth ached, she so longed to gnash them. Doubtless Zeus was stalking some doxy in Seattle. The rescue of Ralph and the reprimand of Ronnie were mere cover stories. The moment she was released she'd fly to Seattle at warp speed and put an end to Zeus' libidinous schemes!

~ ✳ ~

The tall girl in pinstripes—she said her name was Veronica—twisted David's will with telekinetic powers. It had to be something like that, since it was happening again. Helpless, he obeyed as she guided his hand to the whole milk and extra shots of chocolate for her tall skinny double mocha with cinnamon.

She stared at him as he handed her the steaming cup, the steel in her eyes softening after she sipped her drink and repeated what she'd said yesterday: "Perfect. Just like they make it at home."

David mastered his jangled nerves and leaped into the conversational abyss.

"So where is that? Home, I mean?"

She licked a blob of milk foam off her upper lip. "Greece, more or less."

Her smile revealed strong, white teeth.

David studied the counter as he wiped it down, avoiding her analytical gaze. "What brings you to Seattle?"

"Corporate restructure," she said.

He looked up, startled.

Dark eyes flashed angrily at him, as if he didn't have the right to be surprised.

"No offence intended," he blurted. "You just look kind of young for that sort of thing."

Her gaze cooled back to analytical. He could almost see her brain shuffling information like a beefed-up hard drive. Her face brightened, indicating what his psych 101 professor had called an "Aha" moment.

"Of course," she said, with a choppy laugh. "I mean, I'm work-ing on a case study about corporate restructure for my dissertation."

"Cool that you get to study abroad," David said, wondering if he could qualify for a program like that if he went back to college and really applied himself. "Are you going for a masters?"

"That would be a thesis, and I've done that. The dissertation is for my doctoral degree," she said with amused patience. "I might look young for my age, but I'm—twenty-six."

"Wow," David said, impressed. "I bet you'll find a job anywhere you want when you graduate." He cast a sheepish glance at the espresso machine.

Veronica sighed. Her forehead furrowed.

"Dad has different plans for me. He runs the family business and he wants me to take over when he retires."

"Bummer. My dad's a CPA and he wants me to be one, too." David rolled his eyes up toward the striped awning, down to the counter and back to Veronica. "Guess I showed him."

She practically spit out a mouthful of mocha when she started laughing. Her glee took him by surprise and he laughed, too.

"It sounds like we have a lot in common," she said, her smile reaching her eyes.

"If you need any pointers on rebellion, I'm your go-to guy," he said, grinning.

Veronica took out another five and stuffed it in the tip jar. "Thank you, David."

It was thrilling to hear her speak his name, though of course she knew it from the Use Your Bean plastic-coated name tag pinned to his chest. For a nanosecond he thought to ask her when she got off work or researching or whatever she was doing, but logic prevailed. What would she want with a guy who was six years younger, uneducated and several inches shorter than she was?

Instead, he gave a brief nod and said, "Thank *you*."

David watched Veronica walk away, shoulders square, dark hair cascading down her back. Yesterday she'd seemed scary but now he realized she was smart, and stately. She waited at the corner of Third and Madison, shifting her weight from one sandaled foot to the other as she gazed over traffic at the notoriously slow *Don't Walk* sign. Like a lot of people who waited at that corner she lifted a hand and pointed an index finger at the signal, which changed immediately. Great timing, he guessed.

"Ahem."

A balding man in a dark blue suit waited in front of him to place an order.

"Sorry, Jeff," he said, enjoying a barista's privilege of calling a man his dad's age by his first name. "Guess I was day-dreaming. The usual?" he said, watching Veronica cross the street as he pulled a 12-ounce paper cup from the top of the stack and started brewing a double shot of espresso for an Americano with amaretto flavoring.

Jeff turned to watch Veronica, too.

"Interesting," he said, holding his chin between thumb and forefinger. "She's going into the Parthenon Building. I went into the lobby once, just out of curiosity, but it's funny. I can't remember a thing about it. I keep meaning to look up the ownership. I guess it keeps slipping my mind."

"I think it has something to do with corporate takeovers," David said through the steam.

"What does?" Jeff said, turning back toward him.

"Whatever they do in the Parthenon Building," David clarified.

"Huh," said Jeff, his face blank as he reached in his billfold for a five and handed it to David. "I must be spending too much time at the desk or maybe it's the heat. What were we talking about?"

He'd never known Jeff to space out like that. David wondered if he had heat stroke.

"Nothing important," David said, handing change and the cup of espresso back to his patron. Jeff dropped the change into the tip jar as David reached for a bottle of spring water displayed on the counter and handed it to Jeff. "Free of charge for customer appreciation," he said, mourning the two dollars in his tip jar that he'd transfer to the till. "Stay hydrated, and have a great day."

Jeff's expression was quizzical. "Thanks," he said, his lips forming a dim smile before he ambled back toward work.

Weird, David thought. An eagle flying over Third Avenue yesterday, Veronica the will-bending Greek girl altering her mocha order by telekinesis, and a sharp guy like Jeff spacing out. Maybe he was imagining things. Maybe the heat was getting to him, too?

Mom would know what to say about all this but he hadn't had time to call her yet. They hadn't talked in two days and he was really starting to worry. David admitted to himself, with some shame, that the one person he'd most like to see right now was his mother, especially if she offered to buy him dinner.

~ ✶ ~

The weight room at the Downtown Gym echoed with clanking metal, accented by puffing and the wiping away of sweat with nubby white towels. Candy grunted under the extra weight she'd added to the bar she used for squats, desperate to keep her aging thighs firm and cursing the number of reps required to keep toned at the age of three thousand nine hundred and ninety-nine. By the end of the week, even that disgusting age would be history!

"Frickin' four thousand on frackin' Friday," she spat on the last rep. Where had the centuries gone? Her red spandex unitard was holding back more than she cared to acknowledge. Not fat, Zeus forbid—when she felt even marginally sane she realized that. But on days like today she felt like her skin was losing elasticity as fast as a cheap pair of pantyhose. These days she counted it a blessing Jim didn't wear his Coke bottle lenses to bed.

The whole aging thing made her want to cry and the women's locker room, empty for once, offered a refuge. Candy set the shower head to the harshest level of massage. She wept and wailed into the violent, pulsing streams. What happened to the days when reverses of fortune made her want to kick an anvil over the moon instead of sobbing her lungs out? Come Friday, youth was gone.

The little girl inside the small-g goddess hoped fervently Jim would remember the day and the year and make a special fuss. He was a good listener, good at hearing her express needs and wishes even she forgot about over time. But sometimes, when he was way stressed-out busy—

"Frickin' frackin' Ralph!" She screamed at the shower wall. A row of tiles pulled away and clattered to her feet. "Frickin' frackin' audit!"

A snooty voice wafted into the shower room. "Mrs. Smith? Candy? Is everything okay in there?"

"Shit!" Candy yelled under her breath. "Of course, Nadine," she said in a voice as sweet as ground glass. Damn little snoop of an aerobics instructor, what was she doing in here anyway? "Everything's just frickin' peachy."

"Language, Candy."

Why in blazes were people always saying that to her?

"That'll be another five dollars for the UGN fundraiser."

"Put it on my bill, Nadine," Candy growled. She threw open the shower door and grabbed a handful of towels from the pristine stack on a long, low table. "And then you can stick the whole thing up your puny, muscular ass!"

"That's good for a one-week suspension, Mrs. Smith," Nadine retorted as she made a check mark on her clipboard. What kind of frickin' bitch brought a clipboard into a locker room?

"Don't you have a class to teach or something?" Candy snarled as she wrapped a towel turban-style around her dripping hair, pretending not to feel that new feeling of self-consciousness about her naked body.

"You can come back next Thursday," yapped Nadine, undeterred. "I'll notify the front desk." She turned on her cross-trainer encased heel and swept out of the locker room.

Candy sagged onto the bench in front of her locker, exhausted from an encounter that would have left her exhilarated such a short while ago. She bent over to dry her legs and feet, eyes half-closed against the wrinkly texture her inner-thighs had started to show. Everything in her life was going to ruin. How could she get rid of the extra quarter-inch on her waist before Friday without having use of the Downtown Gym?

Candy tore off her turban and hurled it against her locker door. Every day she longed more and more for a baby and why not, since her figure was going to shit in a hand basket? But Jim didn't want to have a baby, he was too stressed to even talk to her about it now. That snoopy little audit snitch was just the icing on the by-Zeus cake!

Tears welled in Candy's eyes. Her mom, Gymnastica (the little-known muse of physical fitness), must have gone through all of this when she was turning four thousand. But Mom and Dad (Pontus, a lesser-known deep sea god) were on a year-long submarine cruise, out of cell phone range. The only other woman she could think of to talk to was her first boss, Hestia, but she was a frickin' frackin' hearth and home virgin! For the first time in her life, Candy sobbed with regret for never having cultivated a female confidant.

When a policeman directed Zeus to the Helping Hearts Soup Kitchen and Shelter, the Lord of the Universe doffed his greasy fedora in thanks. At least his disguise was up to par, but last night—

Last night he'd made a miscalculation. After the elation of going unrecognized by Jim, Zeus had decided to celebrate with a quick flight from Seattle to London to look up Briana. He'd transformed his attire back to a glistening white toga with gold trim for the occasion and hovered near her face molecules in Big Ben's four-sided clock. Anticipating a warm welcome, he'd been nonplused to receive a lightning-quick rebuff from the gorgeous British structureling.

She'd even quoted from the Sexual Harassment section of the Immortal Resources Employee Handbook! He'd returned to Seattle at warp speed, humiliated by her vehement rejection and exhausted from three trans-oceanic flights in less than a day.

But that was yesterday. Today the sky was bright and his schedule was free of bureaucratic boar dung. Tired though he was, Zeus strolled south to Pioneer Square and entered the dingy comfort of the soup kitchen. The coffee the policeman had so thoughtfully recommended was a scorched, medium-bodied blend, well-aged on a grocery store shelf before donation, but the jolt of caffeine was welcome. Too weary to engage in conversation, Zeus listened to the utterances of a small collection of down-at-the-heels men and women and the shelter staff. Yesterday's deluge had created a shortage of cots for those seeking to sleep out of the rain. The staff members nodded with approval at the radio's announcement of highs in the upper eighties with no chance of precipitation.

After a second cup of coffee (laced with an abundance of sugar) Zeus thanked his hosts and strolled northwest, toward the Alaskan Way Viaduct.

For a while he just stood there, staring up at Ralph's eye molecules. Where had the centuries gone, the time since he'd first met Ralph and Briana at a recruiting session at Athens Tech? Twenty-six hundred years ago they'd been the cream of the senior class—Ralph a confident young giant with ambition, Briana intelligent, serious, and blooming with strength and beauty. From the way she carried herself Zeus was aware she was newly pregnant, though she didn't realize it yet. Ronnie was just a baby back then, and Hera hadn't had the time or inclination for husbandly attentions for much too long. He'd turned on the Big-G charm and seduced Briana, knowing the responsibility of paternity wouldn't be his this time. He didn't give the girl much thought in the following centuries, except when he'd been necessarily present to move her from job to job, at which times he naturally pressed his suit. But he'd made a mistake when he transferred her to Big Ben in 1859 AD. He hadn't realized Briana and Ralph had been lovers in college and now Ralph, a mere 2.71 miles distant in the London Bridge, could telepathically communicate with her! Zeus couldn't tap into Ralph's words but he could sense the intent. Briana's replies were cool and aloof, for which Zeus was grateful as it took almost a century of wading through Immortal Resources red tape to get Ralph transferred to Seattle.

The Lord of the Universe felt a twinge of remorse as he looked upon the burnt-out structureling holding up the most wretched piece of architecture on earth. He was Zeus the Thunderer, above such jealousy and the need for hot-blooded revenge! Zeus patted his slight mead-gut, a feature of his build since he'd turned six thousand. He had to end Ralph's insane assignment, but who would be dumb enough to take Ralph's place? Ronnie's half-baked idea of replacing structurelings with computers was sheer, unproven insanity! If she really wanted to help, she should be recruiting some untried Athens Tech senior and offering a signing bonus to take the Alaskan Way Viaduct job.

Annoyed, Zeus turned his head from side to side, looking past the Viaduct and up and down the Seattle waterfront. Where in this small-g city was Ronnie, anyway? The only other god, Big or small, he'd seen in Seattle was Jim, idiotically completing his transformation from pigeon to man in front of a witness! How was such careless-ness possible in a god who'd made Level Seventeen, who'd been Continental Manager of Australia? After Jim had made his incredible transformation blunder, Zeus had watched him stride uphill. Jim had ascended a few blocks and turned left at a street corner. Had Ronnie made contact with Jim? Was he in on her scheme, whatever it was? Had she gone renegade, rallying sympathizers and planning to over-throw her own dad, just as he'd overthrown his father, Cronus?

Zeus told himself it was the soup kitchen coffee souring his gut, not fear of a large-scale rebellion. Keenly feeling his lack of omnisci-ence he turned uphill, following Jim's path in a search for Ronnie. Whatever she was up to, he had to intervene before Ralph and the rest of the world crumbled into a heap of dust!

When Veronica returned to the Smiths' penthouse that morn-ing, Jim answered her knock as quickly as if he'd been on standby and ushered her into the kitchen. He smiled but his eyes looked wor-ried as he poured aerated milk from the frothing pitcher. From the texture of the bubbles topping her mocha, she knew he'd used whole milk this time.

Jim's hands trembled slightly as he handed her the mug and picked up his own. "You can work in my office, if that's all right?" He backed out the kitchen door, an unsupported grin pasted on his face.

"Sounds fine."

Jim looked scared, really scared about something. Who wouldn't be, living with Candy? Veronica resolved to be as friendly as was appropriate in the situation, hoping to put him at ease. If he was too nervous about the audit he might hover and she'd never have a chance to search his client files.

He led her to hallway. The first door to the left opened onto a large, square room with a sparse selection of oversized furnishings. An oak desk, its thick legs carved with ivy vines, and a matching armchair sat to the immediate right, facing a window with a view of the upper floors of Third Avenue skyscrapers. Two beige armchairs and a low table with a plump box of tissues on top looked back toward the desk. The wall to the right of the desk and chairs held a single large canvas, an abstract painting of deciduous trees turning color in the fall. An oak bookcase four shelves high grounded the wall to the left. It was filled with volumes bound in ancient leather and titled in gold, probably the professional library he'd used before he'd been demoted from his Continental Manager assignment. A matching six-drawer file cabinet stood alongside the bookcase. Veronica's eyes fixed on a large Lucite square perched on top. It encased an orange rubber globe covered with black signatures.

"This looks interesting," she said, pointing at the mysterious object and consciously putting a smile in her voice.

"The Seattle SuperSonics," Jim said with reverence. "From the nineteen seventy-nine NBA championship game. I still can't believe I was there! The saddest day of my life was when the team moved to Oklahoma."

Veronica nodded solemnly, as if she understood his cryptic words.

"I've found most of files you requested," he said, his nervous grin returning as he gestured toward three tidy stacks of manila folders on the desk. "I have to unlock our storage space in the basement to get the files from nineteen thirty to nineteen forty-nine. Thank Zeus we only have to file every two decades!"

"Thanks, Jim, and please take your time," Veronica said. She set her briefcase alongside the piles of documents and sat in the carved oak chair, her toes dangling above the floor. "Looking through these will take me a few hours at least."

Jim backed toward the doorway, bobbing and grinning, hands gripping his coffee mug. "If you need anything, just ask!"

She beamed him a relaxed smile. "Thank you, Jim."

The door closed soundlessly behind him.

Veronica regarded the pile of documents representing 1990 through 2009, a stack six inches thick just like the other two. Disgusting waste of storage and inefficient, too. Why Dad wouldn't let go of paper returns and go digital she didn't understand. She'd gleaned and beefed up state-of-the-art mortal digital technology in time for the 2009 filing date and still he hadn't given in!

But the preparation and archiving of tax returns were minor matters compared to the work she'd come to accomplish. Veronica's eyes shifted toward the file cabinet. The top two drawers were marked "regional," the remaining four labeled with intervals of letters in the English alphabet. An entire drawer was dedicated to the letter "R". Though she was confident her structureling reform proposal would improve Ralph's working conditions and personal life beyond his wildest dreams, Dad had taught her plenty about the older generation's resistance to change. It was good policy to have a trump card in hand for leverage, if needed. If the "R" drawer held such a card she'd use it to assure Ralph's cooperation—a loathsome practice of last resort, but sometimes you had to stomp grapes to make wine.

The file cabinet was secured with a small-g repelling spell, a pleasing reassurance her disguise was working. Veronica smiled as she reversed the spell and slid open the "R" drawer.

The drawer was crammed with manila file folders, each one with "Ralph" appearing somewhere on the label. She pulled the personal history and work review files from the front. Hopefully she'd find what she needed without scavenging through dozens of folders of Jim's notes from Ralph's weekly counseling sessions.

Ralph's academic history was more impressive than she'd anticipated. He'd graduated near the top of his class at Athens Tech with a double-major in construction and architectural sciences and a concentration in bridges and public arenas. It took some reading between the lines to figure out why he'd been booted from a choice assignment in London Bridge (years before it was moved to Arizona) and stuck in the architectural armpit he inhabited now, but given Dad's ham-fisted supervisory methods, she wasn't surprised. The notes made it more than clear Dad knew about Ralph's romantic overtures to Briana, the Big Ben structureling who'd been Ralph's college sweetheart.

Veronica sighed and leafed through Ralph's counseling files, starting with 1953. When she approached him for recruitment this afternoon, uncloaked and golden aura blazing, she had to be armed with something that would make him listen, and listen carefully— something Dad didn't already know.

Candy rushed through the penthouse door. Tears welled in her eyes. She vaguely noticed the audit brat's grey pinstripes passing opposite her. Thank Zeus the loathsome little snip was leaving. Candy would explode if she had to wait one more minute to tell Jim she needed a baby—now!

She found the prospective father slumped in his favorite living-room chair, knees on elbows and head in hands. The chair-side reading lamp shone on his bald spot.

"Jim?"

"Hi, honey!" he cried, leaping to his size 18 feet.

Oh shit, he was having a manic melt-down!

"How were things at the gym?" he chirped. Jim grabbed his favorite Sonics mug off the coffee table and took an abrupt slurp. "Whew! That's cold!" He peered into the mug. "Forgot all about it, I guess."

Jim set the mug down with a clank and paced frantically in front of the picture window overlooking Elliott Bay. Candy's head tracked his movements as if she was watching a tennis match.

"Too busy finding our tax records for the auditor, I guess. You should see the files I pulled out of the basement storage for nineteen thirty to nineteen forty-nine—moldy as all get-out! I was so distracted I hardly paid attention to old Henry during his counseling session. Thank Zeus there's never much going on at the Smith Tower. Ha, ha, ha!"

"Jim!" she cried, her heart sinking. It always happened this way. He'd carry on all calm and solicitous of her moods and then out of nowhere he'd snap. Hyperactive babbling was the first sign. She'd have to get him out of here, away from work and all the other crap that was happening to them, get him to relax, but when? He could spin on like this for days!

"I never did finish telling you about the homeless guy yesterday. He caught me in mid-transformation from being a pigeon. Ha, ha, ha! And the funny part is, I didn't even detect his mortal body heat beforehand! Guess I'm losing it."

Jim slumped back into his chair, eyes glazed. "I think the homeless guy might be undercover, maybe a cop," he said in a hoarse whisper. He picked up his mug and sipped again, pausing to smile mechanically and ask again, "So honey, how were things at the gym?"

Candy pushed the tears from her eyes into her throat. She needed Jim to be strong for her more than ever, but until he calmed down it was hopeless. All she could do was shake her head, bolt from the room and lock herself in the master suite to let her tears roll in silence. Her face was a soggy mess by the time she heard a familiar rap on the door.

"Candy? Honey?" Jim said in his high-tension voice. "Don't worry about a thing, Candy. Everything's ninety-nine percent okey-dokey!"

She pulled open her lingerie drawer and dug to the bottom, scrabbling for a Fran's Gold Bar she'd stowed against this very type of emergency. Jim's wild assurances mixed in her ears with the crinkle of gold foil as she unwrapped the chocolate, caramel and almond confection. She licked salt tears from her lips between each sweet, reassuring bite.

~ ✻ ~

Ralph's eye molecules narrowed as he peered up Madison. The girl descending from Third Avenue was immortal, no question—a purple aura emanated from the top of her head. He was pretty sure it was purple. Ralph's color blindness got a little worse every century.

As she crossed Second Avenue he noticed golden rays. A super-aura. Ralph caught his breath, caused the Viaduct to waver as if in a stiff breeze. She was a Big-G!

She had to be the Big-G who'd swooped over him yesterday morning. And even though it hadn't been Zeus, something—Ralph knew to the base of his piers—was going to happen. Something big.

She crossed Western, close enough now so Ralph could distinguish her dark, piercing eyes. One of Zeus and Hera's kids, or maybe one of Demeter's or Poseidon's or Hades'? The pinstripe toga confused him. Had Olympus endowed a Goddess of Accounting?

The Big-G carried a briefcase. With her free hand she shaded her eyes against the early afternoon sun which had started its white-hot western decline. Eyes locked with eye molecules. She introduced herself via direct link to Ralph's mind, her words reaching him from where she stood below, audible in spite of the roar of traffic.

She was the "surprise" baby the small-g gods had gossiped about twenty-six hundred years ago, Veronica by name, a perfect copy of Hera in her youth. With flawless telekinetic diction she told him about a plan, a plan she wanted him to be a part of that involved computers and sounded way too good to be true. Ralph was suspicious of computers. Jim had tried to interest him in them on occasions when they'd had heart-to-heart chats about how quickly the world was changing, but he just couldn't buy in to the digital age.

Ralph told Veronica her plan was crazy. Her expression turned grim. She mentioned, in some detail, a particular incident from his past, an ill-judged antic from senior year at Athens Tech. He'd told Jim about it in an early counseling session when he'd needed to let off some steam about Zeus forcing him into his current crappy assignment. The story was ancient—even his classmates had probably forgotten it by now. Ralph's inner voice tried to change the subject but Veronica wouldn't be swayed, said if he didn't participate in a demonstration that could, among other things, revolutionize his working life, word of the damning incident was going straight to Zeus.

Don't worry about Dad, she thought in response to Ralph's mind blurting "Zeus isn't gonna like this!" *I'll back you, Ralph. Just trust me.*

Her lips pressed into a flat smile, ending the conversation and leaving Ralph with two bad choices. Whether he cooperated with Veronica or whether he didn't, Zeus would kill him!

Day Three: Thursday

If David didn't sacrifice his pride and go to the Food Bank this afternoon he'd die of starvation, or at least he'd feel like he had. Last night he'd given in to the hollow groans of his digestive system, couldn't stop himself from preparing and wolfing his last two boxes of macaroni and cheese like a zombie chomping a brain.

As soon as he'd set up the espresso cart Thursday morning David made himself a large cup of cocoa to get his blood sugar up. He'd lucked out and found an abandoned *Seattle Times* on the bus last night, but the minimum qualifications for jobs that paid well weren't ones he possessed, nor was his boss known for giving good references. Going back to college seemed the only real answer, but he'd been such a flop at it before, and even after eighteen months as a barista he still didn't know what he wanted to do with his life. Except spend a week at an all-you-can-eat restaurant.

David drained the dregs of his cocoa and licked as far down the inner sides of the recycled paper cup as his tongue could reach. The news radio reported smooth traffic with no delays on I-5 or Highway 520. He fidgeted with his cell phone, tempted to call his mom but the morning rush was due to descend any minute. Last night he'd called her several times but no one answered. He'd finally left a message but she hadn't returned it yet. David tried not to worry about her, though scenes of hospitalization or her car broken down in the Utah desert flashed through his mind.

He poked his head through the cart window and looked up and down Third Avenue to reconnoiter the arrival of his patrons. None of his regular suits were in sight yet. He spotted a shabbily dressed guy with flowing white hair half-a-block away.

Please, no, thought David. He saw plenty of homeless people at the bus shelter between Third and Fourth on Pike when he waited for the bus home to the U-District. They didn't usually drift this far into the business district, preferring the retail part of downtown where crowds were larger and the prospect of panhandling a stray buck was greater.

This one looked older than most, maybe seventy judging from the deep crinkles in the corners of his eyes that even David could see from a distance. Maybe he was less than seventy if he was prematurely white and laughed a lot? The man wore a brimmed hat, baggy pants, hobnail boots held to the soles by a few threads and a stained overcoat that looked so old it could have belonged to David's long-dead grandfather.

David willed himself and the espresso cart to become invisible. He didn't have anything against the homeless—to the contrary, he knew himself to be an easy mark. One guy who haunted the bus shelter had given him the nickname "Little Daddy Warbucks" because he couldn't bear to pass anyone who looked hungry without surrendering his pocket change.

The old guy loomed closer, his smile broad. As he swaggered up to the Use Your Bean counter David noticed his teeth were whole and white.

"What can I do for you?" David asked with false cheer. If he gave the lone nickel in his pocket to this guy, others were sure to come. And when they did, given the current condition of his finances he'd be living on the street himself before the end of summer.

The old man's eyes were dark, their expression merry.

"Too early in the day for the grain or the grape." His voice was resonant and pleasant, like the host of a swing music radio show Dad listened to. "What's the fee for a plain cup of dark roast coffee?"

"Fifty cents," David lied, cutting the price by a dollar and a half. If he took the difference out of his tip jar no one would know. He hoped. The boss counted tips daily along with the deposit money and had a keen sense for how much the amount should be. He'd raised an eyebrow yesterday, the day David had taken two dollars for Jeff's "complimentary" bottled water out of the tip jar.

As David pumped twelve ounces of dark roast from the vacuum pot he heard coins jingle in the man's overcoat pocket. David snapped a recycled plastic lid onto the cup and set the brew before his patron.

"I heard a rumor there were some strange things happening around here," the old man said in a lowered voice as he looked to the left and to the right.

"What kind of things?" David asked out of reflexive politeness. It was nearly seven o'clock. He prayed for the conversation to end so the man would go away before the first espresso tsunami of the day hit.

"Things you wouldn't normally see," the man said, leaning closer. He smelled like someone who ate a lot of garlic, not like the bouquet of garbage and urine and fortified wine that reeked off most of the homeless guys. "Unidentified flying objects?" he continued, dark eyes twinkling. "Abrupt changes in weather? Maybe a minor earthquake?" he added in a hopeful tone.

"No, not really," David said, unwilling to prolong the conversation by mentioning the eagle flying down Third Avenue two days ago and the torrential rainstorm later that day.

"Any strangers down this way?" The man continued, tilting an ear toward David as if he expected him to whisper a reply. "Any foreigners? Any aliens?"

The guy was nuts! David nearly told him to get lost, but his mother's voice echoed in his head, reminding him to be compassionate to the less fortunate.

"No, sir, nothing like that down here."

A trickle of summer suits ebbed down the sidewalks toward the espresso stand. Jim, the geek from across the street, emerged from the building he lived in and waved to David. Jim stopped at the crosswalk on the corner of Third and Madison and waited for the light to change. Doubtless he was coming to check the Use Your Bean cookie inventory for his weirdo wife.

"Thanks, son," the old guy said, reclaiming David's attention as he flattened some coins on the stainless steel counter, his hand streaked with dirt but his fingernails trimmed and clean. "Keep the change. And be sure to let me know if you see anything unusual." He winked and spun on his heel, facing the street.

Jim, still holding vigil for the electronic "Walk" icon, swiveled his head toward the homeless man and jumped. All six-foot-eight of him froze for a second. He pantomimed he'd forgotten his wallet and strode back from where he'd come.

As Jim stumbled through the revolving door the old guy burst out laughing. David's first two customers pressed themselves against the espresso cart counter, putting as much distance between themselves and the jovial wino—or maybe he was an undercover agent from the Immigration and Naturalization Service, the way he'd asked about aliens?—as possible.

"Café amaretto and a double-shot with half-and-half coming up," David said to the suits, two of his regulars. Making the order was mechanical after eighteen months, so even the distraction of the old man didn't make him goof up, though it kept him thinking.

Something didn't add up about this guy, and it was the strangest thing David had seen all week.

~ ✳ ~

Jim leaned against the penthouse door, doubled over and panting. He flattened his palm on his chest to contain his heart that leapt like a caged, wild animal. All he'd been trying to do was pick up a little treat at the espresso cart for Candy to give her day a happy start, especially as the auditor had returned at six AM. Things were bad enough—Ralph's emotional upheavals, Candy's ejection from the Downtown Gym, the audit—without crossing paths with the undercover cop masquerading as a wino! What if he'd told the espresso kid about seeing Jim transform from a pigeon to a man? If the auditor somehow learned about this screw-up, he'd be small-g toast!

He used what he could remember about biofeedback to regulate his pulse, just as he had yesterday after he'd babbled to Candy so much she'd locked herself in the bedroom. Veronica was working in his office. He had to appear cool and calm so she wouldn't see his agitation and think it was a red flag indicating something hinky in his tax returns. Jim took a calming breath and manifested the best possible outcome. Miss Zeta would find an innocent error, dun him with a small fine and fly back to the Olympus, Inc., Central Office—today.

This happy scenario held for nearly eight seconds. That's when the penthouse echoed with the clash of hangers from the walk-in closet. Jim sprinted to the master bedroom, thankful the office door was closed. He hoped it was thick enough to keep the auditor from hearing the worst.

"Candy, honey, I—"

"Get out of here with your damn cookies!" she screamed. Candy hurled a pair of red spike-heeled lace-up boots at his chest. "I'm fat! Fat I tell you!" She stood, stark naked, in front of the wall of mirrors she'd had installed when they first moved in decades ago.

"Candy, I never made it to the—"

She pinched and jiggled the very slight fullness of her belly. "After all these centuries, Jim," she said as tears streaked down her face, "after all these centuries you should know when I say I want cookies I really mean I don't!"

Candy threw herself face-down on the vast, round bed and

sobbed into the red velvet coverlet, pummeling her feet on memory foam. Her bottom was as attractive to Jim as ever, even as it quivered in middle-aged agony. He set her boots on a chair and gently closed the door. Thank Zeus he had control of himself today, at least for the moment. One of them had to hold on to sanity, even if it meant taking turns.

Her convulsions crested and fell. She turned over and faced him, her eyes ringed with mascara.

"Four thousand!" she said, shaking her golden curls in disbelief. "I'm going to be four thousand tomorrow, Jim! It's all going to shit," she moaned, pulling the bedspread around her mid-section. "I may as well eat the damn cookies and get it over with."

She held out one hand like a hungry child, begging.

Jim braced himself. "Candy. Honey."

Her magnificent brow furrowed, signaling the storm was far from over.

He bit the inside of his cheek, a nervous habit he fell back on when he wanted to scream but couldn't for professional reasons.

"I don't have any cookies, Candy. I didn't make it across the street."

She raised a skeptical eyebrow.

"The old man was over there, Candy, the wino. The guy who caught me in mid-transformation that I think might be an undercover—"

"You, afraid of a wino?" she said in a tone of disgust. Candy flung herself off the bed and returned to the closet. She rummaged through hanger after hanger of bright red clothing until she came to the most concealing garment she owned—a low-necked, calf-length red cotton dress. "Think about it, Jim. No one's going to believe a crazy story from a wino. They'd assume it was a hallucination."

He wouldn't even try to explain how something about the old man's eyes had made his stomach sore. It hardly mattered, as the world as Jim knew it resumed crashing down around him in spite of his cheerful attempts at denial. He knew he should be keeping tabs on Ralph today but his head was too full of his own anxiety to deal with someone else's problems. He felt foolish and powerless, didn't have heart enough to listen to Ralph's real and serious issues for which he could offer no lasting solution.

Candy, now dressed and accessorized with matching high-heeled sandals and purse, brushed past him.

"I'll buy the damn cookies if you're afraid to, Jim."

The way she said his name sounded like a knife twisting in raw meat but he lacked the emotional strength to tell her so. The staccato click of heels ticked across the entryway floor. The penthouse door opened and slammed. Sick to death of ceaseless tension, Jim retreated to the bathroom cabinet in search of antacid.

Down the hall in Jim's office, Veronica, too, felt ill. Frozen at the window, she stared down at Third Avenue. While standing at the file cabinet to review Clifford's files she'd noticed a disheveled man with flowing white hair talking to David at the espresso cart across the street. She'd always been able to see through Dad's disguises, ever since Mom showed her a nifty little trick about penetrating Zeus' Biggest of Big-Gs cloaking. Did Dad know she was in Seattle, too? If not, what was he doing here, especially so close to fiscal year-end?

Veronica shook herself from her trance. Someone must have ratted on her, but who? She hadn't even told her neighbor who was taking care of Bill Gates, Jr., where she was going, or why. She'd have to work fast before Dad stopped her and her whole plan fell apart. Veronica tiptoed to the penthouse door and made a quiet exit. Too upset to cloak, without which she dared not fly, Veronica opted to sneak out the building's back entrance, catch the next Monorail to Seattle Center and have a timely heart-to-heart with the Space Needle.

~ ✳ ~

"I am one lucky bastard," Cliffie said to himself every morning at sunrise, his eye molecules taking in north, south, east and west as the upper deck of the Space Needle slowly rotated. The town had really grown since the 1962 World's Fair but Seattle Center was a lonely place for a structureling. There were lots of buildings but, except for the Space Needle, no one was needed to hold them in place. Even Paul Allen's wildly curving EMP Museum could stand on its own, thanks to late twentieth century engineering advances.

There was no one to talk to. He hadn't even talked to Mum since Zeus brought him here in 1962 during the final phases of construction. Jim, of course, visited him once a week for counseling, but that was merely required corporate routine. Thank Zeus he'd insisted on a provision in his employment contract that he be kept up-to-date on mortal computer technology. Jim had faithfully brought updates and recorded Cliffie's evolving structureling technology theories, but even with this teamwork they'd never achieved a personal rapport. They were simply of different generations.

Cliffie sighed. At least Jim was aware of his existence. The daily multitudes of mortal visitors didn't know about Clifford Essex, the most intellectually gifted structureling in his graduating class, though they continually praised the Space Needle.

But this week something exciting had happened. The Big-G who had flown in and circled him several minutes on Tuesday morning hadn't said anything, but he'd gotten a good look at her while he pretended to sleep. Cliffie's heart molecules raced. Maybe he was being observed for a reason. Maybe, just maybe, his first official structureling stint was coming to an end and he was up for promotion!

Whoever she was who'd observed him hadn't come by during business hours, hadn't seen the vast volume of traffic he could handle. Summer was his season of glory, with tourists and even locals flocking to ride his three elevators up to the heavens. In summer it didn't matter if it was Thursday mid-morning (as it was at the moment)—he was swamped! Maybe he'd get a chance at the Eiffel Tower job. Probably too much to hope for, but Reginald was older than any other structureling Cliffie knew. Reginald had to retire one day, had to get re-materialized by Zeus one last time and regain his human form. If Cliffie snagged the Paris assignment, maybe he could visit Mum in London on the way!

Cliffie sensed a shimmer of warmth circling him. Oh joy, the Big-G was back! She—someone roughly his own age dressed in a grey pin-striped toga—de-cloaked on a section of his deck that was closed for maintenance, deserted as the crew had gone to an early lunch. In one hand she held a briefcase. She widened her mouth to a serious smile full of strong, white teeth.

"Clifford Essex, I presume? I'm Veronica Zeta."

Her dark eyes and luxuriant hair dazzled him. She was handsomely tall by human standards. Cliffie tried to recall his own height, when reconstituted. Would they look good together?

"My pleasure," he said, his British accent obvious against her perfectly enunciated and unaccented English. One of his girders trembled ever-so-slightly, his hand molecules tempted to reunite and take hers.

"Mr. Essex—may I call you Clifford?"

"Of course," he said. One of the three elevators hiccupped for a split second, his heart molecules racing with joy.

"Clifford, I'm Zeus and Hera's youngest child, and I'm as much on the horns of a dilemma as a Minoan bull-leaper."

She had a sense of humor, too! All three elevators slowed to a stop. The squeals of the encapsulated tourists jogged him back to reality. He breathed slowly in and out, using the relaxation technique Jim had coached him in for moments of great emotion. Ah, if only he were free of structureling responsibility for the evening and could invite her to dinner!

"Long story short, I'm looking for an ally. I'm supposed to run Olympus, Inc., when Dad retires. Quite frankly," she said, lowering her voice and looking around to assure their privacy, "he's not very good at organizational matters and the company's a mess. I'm in Seattle to demonstrate an efficiency reform, one that involves you."

His heart molecules slowed with disappointment. The elevators jerked, eliciting another round of screams, and continued the crawl toward their destinations. The divine Miss Zeta was here on business, too, just like Jim. But oh-so-much prettier.

"How may I be of assistance, Miss Zeta?" Her love, he realized, was not to be his, at least for the present, but swift brain molecules recognized the advantage of helping the future CEO.

"I've reviewed your personnel files, Clifford, and I'm impressed with your academic record at Athens Tech, particularly your dissertation on 'Structureling Future: Scenarios of Centuries to Come.' I'm hoping you'll help me demonstrate one of your ideas for Zeus. I need to show him how operations can be streamlined and how Immortal Resources can be used to optimal advantage."

The paint on Cliffie's upper girders rose in infinitesimal blisters. "Certainly," he said, warmed with pride. She respected his intelligence, a good place to start. His lonely, boring life transformed, Cliffie's—make that Clifford's—foolish heart urged him to dream up new ways to impress the flawless Veronica Zeta on her next visit.

"Terrific!" she said, flashing her magnificent teeth and smiling with her eyes, too. "Just one more thing." She paused and moved her head from side to side again in search of possible eavesdroppers. "If you see Zeus, don't breathe a word about this," she whispered. "Surprise is of the essence!"

Clifford's molecules froze. The mere thought of a visit from Zeus stunned him. He couldn't even collect himself to say goodbye when the divine Veronica Zeta vanished under her cloak and soared away.

~ * ~

Attempting to relax between rush hours, Ralph tried, and failed, to clear his mind. The impulse to escape the Alaskan Way Viaduct was close to irresistible. His efforts to overcome the urge that would kill himself and hundreds of innocent mortals weakened with each clash of tire on metal plate.

Where in Heaven and Earth was Jim? He'd said on Tuesday he'd be back to visit on Wednesday, but Wednesday was gone. If Ralph could only talk to someone who cared about him a little bit he knew he could hold on for another day.

Ralph screamed in unison with the arriving Bainbridge Island ferry's whistle, gaining miniscule relief for his molecules which felt funny today, kind of thick and lightly magnetized. The last rush hour of the day was pending. He tried again, breathing slowly in and slowly out, pondering with each breath the meaning of the phrase *the reward of relaxation is relaxation.*

~ * ~

Hera's stone prison dissolved the instant the 48-hour spell expired. The fire of irritation that had sparked inside her for two days blazed to an inferno.

"Zeuuuuus!"

Marble columns trembled at the thunder in her voice. She strode from room to room in their Mount Olympus condo, bellowing his name. He wasn't in the bathroom (for a change), not in his office, not sniffing around the kitchen for a fresh bag of bore rinds. She flung open the door to his private bedchamber and grunted in irritation to find the silk-covered bed undisturbed. The door to the left was open, revealing their shared connubial suite. The solid gold doorknob was polished to a bright finish. For a moment Hera faltered, remembering the days when that same knob was perpetually smeared with Zeus's fingerprints. Sighing, she entered the chamber, glad she'd ordered the housekeeper to keep it clean and ready for use. Dust covers in the marital suite would be too, too depressing.

The outer wall of the suite was floor-to-ceiling windows. Starlight (which had been burning since Zeus had charged off) cast a silver glow over the remarkably large and comfortable bed, the wardrobe, the vanity table. A scroll of parchment lay on the table.

"Hmmmm," she rumbled to herself. Hera settled on the carved vanity stool and unrolled the message that, she was certain, would fail to please.

Dearest Wife, Doubtless you are beyond fury with me, but as CEO of Olympus, Inc., Hah! Hiding behind his title, the coward! *it is incumbent upon me to find out what our headstrong youngest is doing and put a stop to it before Seattle falls into Puget Sound. As Ronnie is little more than a child I expect to have the matter resolved before you awake, but, if not, know that I am soon to return home. Yours celestially, Zeus*

"Little more than a child!" Hera raged to the empty room. "Your big, fat, stupid ego never could accept that any of our children could be as important as you! First you convince Ronnie to be your successor, then you won't let her take the reins!"

Ronnie was capable of overseeing the earth, even at the young age of twenty-six hundred. Hera had recognized her youngest daughter's intellect, discipline and imagination centuries ago. Who had critiqued the girl's master's thesis before the final draft? Who knew what Ronnie had in mind for modernizing and streamlining operations, the topic of her doctoral dissertation?

"*Not* her father!"

Hera mashed Zeus' note into a ball and pitched it out the open window like so much trash, watching as it tumbled into darkness and disappeared from sight. Like it or not, her life was inextricably tied to Zeus'. Their marriage was in the slops jar, a painful admission for the Goddess of Marriage, but personal considerations would have to wait. First she had to rescue Olympus, Inc., from the brink of operational ruin. She'd follow Zeus to Seattle and bind him with charmed ropes if necessary to make him listen to Ronnie!

Veronica settled into the stack of feather pillows on her hotel bed, sandals off and feet up. The day had been long enough without spotting Dad and having to rush her plans for the demonstration.

Personnel issues were her least favorite part of business administration and recruiting Clifford had made her nervous. She hadn't expected him to speak with an English accent, but then, candidates for advanced structureling studies drew small-g giants from all over the world. Veronica kicked herself for not guessing. She'd read in Clifford's file that his mom was Briana, the Big Ben small-g.

That same Briana had ended up being the key to blackmailing Ralph. The two of them shared an irreverent sense of humor which had come into play when they were co-chairs of the Athens Tech Senior Glee Night. They'd written and starred in a sketch depicting Dad as a cuckold, with Ralph kneeling in his portrayal of Zeus to adjust for the height difference. At first this discovery had amused Veronica but when she realized the timing was shortly after her own date of birth...But no, Dad was the cheater, not Mom. They'd simply turned reality on its head to create comedy.

"I must be getting slow," she said to the empty suite.

Veronica reached into her briefcase that lay next to her, pulled out her laptop, pressed the "power" button and started keying in details from her meeting with Clifford. His dissertation was an integral part of the demonstration she hoped to pull off, Dad willing. Clifford had developed a theory that married structureling intellectual strength and physical endurance to mortal technology. Through his contractual stipulation to be kept up to date on technological advances he'd revised his earlier work to incorporate the digital age and nanotechnology.

Her eyelids fluttered and her fingers slipped off the keys. Veronica saved her changes, set the laptop aside and snuggled sideways into the pillows, wishing Bill Gates, Jr.'s, furry orange warmth was beside her. If Dad hadn't shown up today she wouldn't have freaked out and been unable to cloak. She could have flown to her interview with Clifford instead of traveling mortal-style from downtown to Seattle Center. Once she'd arrived she'd had to wait until 10 AM to give Clifford a chance to adjust to mortal activities at the start his work day. This turned out to be a blessing as it gave her time to recover composure enough to cloak, though she'd had to hide behind a hedge to enable the cloaking to avoid drawing the attention of the mortal tourists.

The promising interview with Clifford had lifted her spirits so much she'd had the energy to enable Biggest of Big-Gs cloaking for the return trip. The short flight to her digs at the Fairmont Olympic accentuated the stiffness she'd earned on the Athens to Seattle run. It would have been so much easier to do overseas travel at warp speed, but Dad wouldn't give her the power until she finished her doctoral degree. Every muscle in her body ached. She'd take a nap, then have a long, hot soak in the goddess-sized bathtub and cuddle up in the complimentary white terry cloth robe with a half-bottle of wine.

Asleep, Veronica manufactured dreams filled with wild extrapolations from the information she'd gathered in Seattle. Candy, having made herself forty feet tall, stomped down Third Avenue causing David, the espresso kid, to run for his life to the Alaskan Way Viaduct, only to find Ralph's shoulders emerging from the upper deck, concrete and steel tumbling perilously to the ground below. Jim watched the spectacle from Clifford's observation deck, sipping a cup of Earl Gray tea, while Dad flew up and down the Seattle skyline swearing and pelting the others with tax returns that hadn't been signed.

But Zeus was not flying up and down the Seattle skyline. He'd materialized alongside Veronica's bed.

Zeus had sensed his wayward daughter's presence the moment she'd emerged from the back entrance of Jim's Parthenon Building. She hadn't cloaked, she'd merely concealed her golden super-aura. It was child's play, tracking her movements to young Cliffie at Seattle Center, which Zeus opted to do remotely. He'd divided his mind's eye in to split screens and roosted on a half wall near the espresso cart to observe Jim's handsome but unbalanced wife, Candy, at the same time he followed Veronica. As Candy approached the rig and bought a handful of chocolate chip cookies Zeus happily remembered the days when Hera had been a raven-haired version of the ravishing blonde.

This recollection screeched to a halt when Zeus' internal vision of Veronica went black. Where had she gone after she left the Space Needle? His throat nearly burst with acid reflux. How could he lose track of her? He'd never taught her top secret Biggest of Big-Gs cloaking. The only possible explanation—his inner eye had somehow failed! When her image returned to the half-screen he nearly fainted with relief. Veronica was striding through the Fairmont Olympic Hotel lobby.

She was easy to find because she hadn't cloaked herself before falling asleep. It was the same mistake she'd made eight centuries ago when she'd run off without permission to see the restoration of the Great Wall of China. They'd argued about the practice of immortals cloaking from other immortals for centuries, Veronica most recently asserting a healthy corporation should strive for transparency in all things. Zeus smiled, remembering her frustrated retort when he'd last broached the subject: "Dad, cloaking is *so* Trojan Horse!"

His paternal heart beat warm but heavy. Free for the past two days from the constant harping of the petty bureaucrats infesting the Olympus, Inc., Central Office, Zeus wondered afresh if it was time to retire. The modern world, with all its policies and regulations, with the bizarre and impractical value it placed on openness, wasn't his cup of mead.

Heaven and Earth, he could use a drink! In lieu of Dionysus, Zeus foraged quietly in the stocked bar in Ronnie's suite. He settled on a half-bottle of Washington-vintage merlot. Zeus leaned back in a padded arm chair with one eye trained on Ronnie, poised to make his escape if she stirred. He almost enjoyed the rare opportunity to sip wine (straight from the bottle in keeping with his disguise) and contemplate his future.

His marriage was the thorniest issue. Centuries had grown few and far between when Hera excited his husbandly desires. He'd given up that part of their marriage completely sometime during nineteenth century AD. In today's world, he pondered, perhaps the romantic options of Lord of the Universe weren't as plentiful as they'd once been? Political correctness had banded his wings—Briana's rebuff had made that clear enough. Was it also possible—he hated to entertain the idea, but—was it also possible that age had muted his appeal? If he tried to rekindle the flame with Hera would she, too, reject a white-haired god of sixty-four hundred with a slight mead gut?

Zeus sipped in grim contemplation. Something had to change. Indeed, much had to change. He swore by the River Styx he'd give his best effort to renew his romantic interest in Hera. But first he had to resolve the crisis with Ronnie. If her in-house revolution succeeded with the structurelings, the best achievement of his career, it would be a hard blow.

Zeus chewed the thought. When the last drops of the half-bottle were drained he still couldn't find his way out of the Olympus, Inc., maze.

DAY FOUR: FRIDAY

Ralph's night-long attempt to gain serenity proved a complete and utter failure. Friday dawned on his muzzy head molecules, finding him unable to decide his course of action. Was it better to take part in Veronica's crazy demonstration and incur Zeus' wrath, or to definitely face Zeus's wrath and possible exile to who-knew-where when the blackmail information came out about Ralph and Briana's highly unflattering Senior Glee Night sketch? If he could only talk it over with Jim—

Ka-chunk, ka-chunk, ka-ka-ka-boom!

"Ouch-ooch-ouch-gheez-oh-shi . . ."

The damn commuters were really pouring it on this morning. The molecules in Ralph's back felt positively bruised from the bumping and thumping. He was thankful his teeth molecules were spread far apart—the constant vibration would have crumbled them by now if they'd been properly intact. If he could just get a break, even for a little while. . . .

Preoccupied with physical and emotional agony, Ralph didn't notice the molecules of his right big toe moving closer and closer together until—

Kabang!

The Viaduct shifted a fraction of an inch. A Ford Taurus and an F-150 pickup side-swiped each other. Two dense lanes of traffic ground to a halt.

The blasts of horns and mortal shouting were deafening. Ralph cast his eye molecules down, his back molecules braced against the immobile deadweight of Detroit. At street level he sighted something terribly, terribly wrong.

"Holy shi—!"

His right big toe wiggled in salute, one hundred times bigger than life and complete with toenail fungus.

"Cool sculpture," a young mortal male with spiked hair remarked as he passed the street-level podiatric pylon.

Ralph's heart molecules beat a wild tattoo. He struggled to recall his relaxation technique. If he could pull himself together—or rather, apart—enough to keep the rest of his molecules dispersed, it would be nothing short of a miracle. And if not? Loss of human life was inevitable, and without a Big-G on hand to reconstitute his molecules into human form when the Alaskan Way Viaduct crumbled and fell, his life, too, would end.

~ ✳ ~

"I'm fat! Fat, fat, fat!!!"

Candy glowered at herself in front of the wall of mirrors, jabbing her belly with the sharp red nail of her right index finger. Tears transformed her mascara into a cosmetic mudslide.

She'd heard about belly fat, loss of skin elasticity and all that other crap small-g women complained about when they arrived at a certain age, but those women didn't take care of themselves. Was it fair for her to suffer the same fate as those lazy cows?!

Candy turned sideways, then backwards, peering over her shoulder into the reflection. At least her butt hadn't gone to pot. *Not yet, anyway* sneered a nasty little voice inside her head. At least she hadn't sprung her hips bearing Jim's children. But now….

A skyscraper's worth of emotional bricks buried her in a heartbeat.

"I want a ba-a-a-by!" she screamed through her tears before collapsing on the vast, round bed, her face in her hands.

All summer she'd tried to bring up the subject, but Jim kept deflecting her overtures. Centuries ago he'd made it clear he didn't want to have children because he didn't know anything about being a father, didn't even know who his own father was. His mom, a retired Muse who knew how to keep a secret, had raised him on her own. Jim's views had made perfect sense when Candy was young and had millennia of child-bearing years ahead of her, but now the hands of her biological clock raced forward like contestants in a chariot race!

What kind of a sick joke birthday was this, anyway? Four frickin' thousand years old, her waist another eighth of an inch bigger when she'd checked her measurements this morning, and Jim unwilling to give her the one thing she wanted most for her birthday. He wouldn't even discuss it! All he'd said to her this morning was something about "that time of the month," which she'd refuted with lightning speed. Candy lunged for a red satin decorative pillow and hurled it at the mirror. The skin on her upper arm wobbled.

"Shit!"

She stormed to her cavernous walk-in closet, trampling en route the sleeveless red mini dress she'd planned to wear today. Candy yanked a section of hangers sideways and shuffled through a series of red dresses in more modest styles. Grumbling, she selected a red sheath with a low-cut neckline (thank Zeus her tits hadn't started a wild ride toward her navel—yet) and long bell sleeves. Once dressed, she viewed the results in the mirror.

Cleavage-youthful and impressive; legs-displayed to advantage by a short hemline; waist-not obviously three-eighths of an inch bigger than perfect. Once she repaired her mascara Candy had to admit she looked damned good.

But she was famished!

She tossed and kicked discarded shoes and clothing aside in search of her purse. It was damned annoying small-gs couldn't conjure such things as mortal money out of thin air. She needed chocolate, and needed it now!

Candy strode to the foyer a split second before the doorbell rang. She flung open the door, hard enough to spring one of the hinges, and bombed past the Audit Girl nitwit on the other side, who at least had the sense to jump out of the way. Candy crossed her forearms and tapped her fingertips furiously against her biceps, waiting for the glacially slow elevator (why didn't Jim do something to make it work faster?). *Oh fricking spare me* she thought when she heard her spouse of two thousand years making conciliatory remarks to Veronica Whatever-Her-Name-Was. Like Candy didn't have the right to do whatever she wanted on her own birthday, especially on her four-thousandth birthday?

The elevator chime pinged at the same instant the penthouse door closed. Candy stepped into the elevator as the bad news hit her—Jim hadn't even wished her Happy Birthday!

She sagged against the elevator wall, stunned. How could all this other shit be going on and her marriage be on the rocks, too? She had to get away from the penthouse, clear her mind and get her shaking hands on some chocolate!

~ ✳ ~

Jim vaulted from the living room sofa and dashed to the hallway when he heard the commotion. The sight of the sprung door, a wide-eyed Veronica and the elevator doors opening for Candy in all her fury drenched him in a cold sweat.

"Zeus on a crutch!" he swore. "Ms. Zeta, I'm so sorry about all this. Please don't take Candy's actions personally. She seems to be going through a challenging time."

Jim watched the girl roll her eyes. *Everything is ninety-nine percent okey-dokey* said his conscious mind as he forced a weak smile.

Veronica Zeta, auditor, reached up and patted him on the shoulder. "It's okay, Jim, really. I'm almost used to it at this point."

Jim studied her expression as he forced the door shut. Ms. Zeta looked tired—and worried. Why would an auditor be worried? It was a curious state of affairs.

"At least let me offer you some coffee," Jim said, tilting his head toward the kitchen.

He could use some too. Jim took his position at the espresso machine with the anticipation of starting a task he knew he was capable of finishing. Candy had been raging more than ever since she'd been suspended from the gym. Last night he hadn't slept. Every time he'd started to drift she heaved an enormous sigh and yanked him back to consciousness. The first several times he'd prompted Candy to say what was bothering her. After a while he couldn't think of new ways to ask the question. Using history as a guide, he knew she'd get even more agitated if he repeated himself so he kept his mouth shut. Candy had dozed just before dawn, muttering in her sleep about a baby as she had every night for a month. Her subconscious thoughts grated on him. Maybe she'd back off when she opened her birthday present today. Jim's psyche winced. Would he prove equal to the resolution he'd made when he'd ordered the gift from the smallgbooksandmore.com website?

Ms. Zeta slumped on a kitchen stool while he prepared the espresso. He eyed her reflection in the stainless steel range hood, watched her head droop ever-so-slightly. The quality of the light around her changed. A bright halo of gold danced above her purple aura.

Holy Zeus, she's a Big-G!

Jim blinked twice and looked again to confirm the observation. He caught his own reflection in the range hood and turned his back to her to conceal his color-drained face.

"One tall skinny double mocha with cinnamon coming up," he said, his brain spinning. Only one ancient line produced Big-G Gods with that type of aura. They were borne of the children of Cronus and Rhea. Jim considered the parental options: Demeter, Poseidon, Hades—but their offspring were of his and Candy's generation. Veronica Zeta must be the "surprise" baby he'd heard about millennia ago. He felt her dark eyes on his back. The comingled gaze of Zeus and Hera made his spine tingle with fear and wonder. What was one of their children doing here, in his Seattle penthouse, masquerading as a small-g bureaucrat?

Jim finished off her espresso drink with whole milk, two extra shots of chocolate and a healthy dash of cinnamon.

"Sorry again about Candy," he said, handing the mug to Veronica. "Family dynamics can be pretty tough to navigate sometimes, especially when people are going through changes they don't want to make."

"Tell me about it," Veronica said, sighing. For once she looked less than perfectly composed and more like a normal twenty-something-hundred-year-old. She sipped her mocha. "You should see my Dad," she continued. "He's had my whole life planned from the start. I'm supposed to take over the family business from him one day, but now I'm ready and he can't stand to give up control."

"Um. Uhuh." Jim listened with full attention as he made his Americano, ninety-nine percent certain the box of tissues in his office was going to be lighter in a very short while. Maybe for Veronica Zeta, daughter of Zeus and Hera, talk therapy would make a real difference.

~ ✳ ~

Tartzilla didn't usually appear this early in the morning, right around 8 AM when the suits had just settled into their high-rise cubicles until coffee break. She was approaching fast, cleavage thrust forward like a figurehead on a clipper ship, bizarrely long red sleeves flapping behind her like warning flags. David fought the impulse to drop to the floor of the espresso cart and fold into the fetal position under the stainless steel sink. He eyed his new inventory of double-dark chocolate chip cookies half-dipped in white chocolate, delivered by Mary the Cookie Lady minutes ago. One dozen, individually wrapped, rested innocently in a low wicker basket on the stainless steel counter. Mary only made the Double-Darks on Friday; competition at 10 AM would be fierce and tips would be hot.

David grabbed the rim of the basket, determined to hide the cookies under the counter to protect his earnings potential, but either he was moving like he was underwater or Tartzilla travelled faster than the speed of light because before he moved an inch her hand was locked on his wrist. Red cupid-bow lips yelled, "Not so fast, shrimp!"

She half-pulled him across the counter, his cell phone banging in the back pocket of his Dockers. Even if he had the chance to punch 911 the dispatcher would laugh him or herself silly if David reported a woman buying all his primo cookies.

David felt a bruise spreading along his left ribs. His free hand released the rim of the cookie basket to feel for bodily damage. For a second he closed his eyes to block tears of pain. When he opened them, the psycho-bitch had released his wrist and was shoveling the last two Double-Darks into her capacious purse.

"Hey!" The guttural quality of his voice barely registered as his own.

She bunched her shoulders like a lioness poised to strike and snarled. Her steel blue eyes blazed savagely as she cursed at him, though he didn't understand the language. The woman—Candy was the name he'd give the police—smashed the purse full of cookies to her chest in a defiant embrace. But in a heartbeat some other emotion swept over her, suspicion maybe, followed by a whimper. One hand slid to rest on her very slightly rounded belly as a single tear rolled down her cheek.

Candy started muttering, her eyes looking nowhere. David could make out something about "four thousand" and "oh fuck!" as her words picked up pace and clarity.

She was ranting, very likely dangerous. What could he—

"M'am? Candy?"

He waved his hands in front of her eyes but she was truly somewhere else. Where was that Jim guy when he needed him? David didn't even have a phone number, but then, why would he? His whole relationship with them was about cookies! He dug in his back pocket for his cell phone, out of ideas except to call 911.

By the time he'd opened the clamshell she'd snapped back to consciousness, her face flushed with anger. Candy slung her purse over her shoulder with violence.

"He didn't even say Happy Birthday!" she screamed, arms thrown wide and hands palm-side-up as if she'd explained it all. She turned and darted between the sparse traffic moving along Third Avenue.

David stood stunned and silent. By the time she reached the street corner opposite and started the descent toward the waterfront, an alarm went off in his head.

She's stealing my cookies! She's stealing my goddamn cookies!

He knew he shouldn't leave the cart but the adrenaline coursing through him couldn't be contained by stainless steel and a striped awning. David hastily switched off the power, slid the window closed and locked the cart door behind him. *Losing forty-two dollars of cookies is bad enough*, his dad's voice hammered in his brain, *it's the principle of the thing! Besides,* Mom chimed in cerebrally, *you can't let that poor, crazy woman roam the streets!*

~ * ~

Hera was annoyed. She'd spent hours looking for Zeus before she thought to employ that stupidly simple trick for penetrating his Biggest of Big-Gs cloaking, which naturally he would have enabled to prevent Ronnie from sensing his presence. Early Friday morning she spoke the words of revealing and within minutes sighted him roaming around under the Alaskan Way Viaduct. She watched from the safety of her own Biggest of Big-Gs cloaking, sneered at the paper bag encased bottle he carried but never took a sip from, his stride buoyant and perfectly straight. Some master of disguise! At least he wasn't with a woman, which, considering the mead gut his tattered overcoat failed to conceal, made perfect sense.

She shoved aside personal vanity in the interest of outdoing Zeus' costume, even if it made her look like stable droppings warmed-over. How liberating it would be to free herself from the old-fashioned "Big-G" look Zeus had insisted she maintain since their marriage forty-six hundred (and sometimes it felt like forty-six thousand) years ago. No more pure white toga edged with gold, goodbye to hours in the salon to renew the braids and curls of her ancient Athens "do." The Goddess of Marriage was primed to give as good as she got!

~ * ~

Zeus held a bottle (the empty he'd drained in Ronnie's suite the night before, covered with a paper bag) by the neck as he stared forlornly at Ralph's materialized toe. Gone were the days when he, Zeus, had built all large architectural structures and had the smarts to make them function as designed. And structurelings, the brilliant fix he'd created and applied to mortal engineering ineptitude, was now rated by Ronnie as mere dressing on a wound that required major surgery! Did she ever stop to consider he'd had to think fast and brilliantly, work tirelessly for centuries reinforcing mortal-made behemoth temples, bridges and skyscrapers that menaced the landscape? And now his brilliant solution to the problem, as personified by Ralph, was literally about to crumble. Thank Heaven and Earth the toe was gigantic and not compressed to Ralph's true scale—somehow he'd managed to stabilize his molecules and halt the process, or so Zeus hoped. He could use some time to think! He had the power to disburse structureling molecules into mortal architectural nightmares and could also extract them and reconstitute them to humanoid form, but what to do about a structureling who'd started re-emerging on his own?

The question gave Zeus a rare and grinding headache. He'd have to blow his cover and reveal himself to Ralph to figure out what to do. Worse yet, disabling his top secret Biggest of Big-Gs cloaking would immediately signal Ronnie that he was in Seattle.

But there was no other choice. Zeus set the bottle on the pavement and stood erect, eyes closed and shoulders back. He took a deep breath—

"You old fool! I knew I'd find you here!"

Zeus nearly jumped out of his overcoat when the screech thundered behind him. He turned, his abruptly opened eyes meeting Hera's.

"Woman, you'll be the mortality of me!" he shouted, alarmed that she'd followed him to Seattle but more so because she'd seen through his top secret Biggest of Big-Gs cloaking.

"Who'll bring in the stars?" he sputtered. "Our electricity bill will be through the roof!"

Zeus eyed Hera's disguise with envy. Twenty-first century cast offs was her theme, a faded floral muumuu accessorized with waffle stompers and a plaid jacket. Her hideous bird's nest of braids and curls was hidden underneath a stained pale pink turban. Her only cosmetic, bright red lipstick, bled onto perfect white teeth.

"You should have thought of that before you trapped me in stone, big-shot!" she shot back. "You and your field work!" Hera raised her arms, burdened with tattered shopping bags. "Would it kill you to pick a disguise that isn't so dowdy? Why not masquerade as a businessman, or even a taxicab driver?"

"Too obvious. Those people have formal networks," Zeus fibbed. He'd learned a thing or two about the homeless network when he'd passed a group of panhandlers at the Pine Street bus shelter. These people did, in fact, know each other and he'd been pertly advised to find his own spot to solicit if he didn't want trouble.

"I'm dealing with a crisis here," Zeus asserted, pointing to Ralph's re-materialized toe. Hera gasped in horror and swung her heaviest bag at Zeus's mid-section.

"Idiot!" she bellowed as he hopped back from the intended blow. "This never would have happened if you'd only taken Ronnie seriously. If she hadn't run away from Athens U to show you whatever it is she's trying to show you, this never would have happened!"

A streak of golden curls, flame red dress and platform sandals rushed close by, knocking Hera on her behind.

"Damn Me!" Zeus cursed, recognizing Candy and her roiling purple aura. Had the whole immortal world gone mad?

"Stop gawking at that tart and help me up!" Hera barked, rolling on the pavement, her legs trapped in the folds of her muumuu. A square-shouldered shadow drifted over her. Zeus looked up at the blue uniform and the badge, up to the face of a sturdy young policeman.

"Okay you two, that's enough roughhousing. Break it up and move along."

Hera, eyes narrowed, struggled to her knees and moved her hands into position to vaporize the lawman.

"Beg your pardon, officer," Zeus said. He touched the brim of his hat, grabbed Hera's elbow and hoisted her to her feet, impressed his wife of four thousand-plus years still had homicidal urges. "The missus was just having one of her seizures. I'll take her over to the Helping Hearts Soup Kitchen for a cup of coffee, that'll set her straight."

"You do that, pal. And no more trouble from either of you," the officer said, shaking his finger in admonishment.

The policeman strolled to the crosswalk. They watched him while he waited for the traffic lights to change, watched him saunter across the street to the waterfront.

"I could kill you for interrupting my spell," Hera said under her breath. "You should have let me blast him!"

"Beauty is as beauty does," Zeus said in a tut-tut tone.

"Like you'd know, in that get-up," she said, looking him up and down, her nose wrinkling in disgust. "As long as I'm not going to let you out of my sight, could we please pick a more attractive disguise?"

"We can talk about that over coffee," he said. Zeus tilted his head in the direction of the soup kitchen several blocks south in Pioneer Square. Her elbow still in his grip, he tugged her into a walk. "Just a curious question, wife," he said, finding the last word more exhilarating than he had any time in recent memory. "How were you able to penetrate my top secret Biggest of Big-Gs cloaking?"

"Oh that," she said, taking her turn with the tut-tut tone. "It's very simple, husband. You talk in your sleep."

Zeus barely checked himself from stumbling. Perhaps she'd tailed him throughout the centuries, witnessed every one of his foolish escapades? Even if she hadn't, dawn was breaking on the idea there was more to Hera than he realized.

David arrived at the foot of Madison Street gut-achingly winded. He braced a hand against a pier of the Alaskan Way Viaduct, glad to feel the cool concrete under his hot, sweaty palm. Scanning the street he saw the old homeless guy (*not* a wino, he'd finally decided after pondering the perfect teeth and lack of urine smell) with a bag lady of similar age, strolling south beneath the raised highway. Across Alaskan Way, seated on a bench near the fire station, David spied the Double-Dark cookie thief.

Still short of breath from his downhill sprint, he passed under the Viaduct and started to cross the street against the light, but retreated to his previous position at the hindmost concrete pier when he noticed a policeman strolling past Ivar's Fish Bar directly across Alaskan Way. They were hell on ticketing jay-walkers downtown. Enough had gone wrong this morning without adding a big, fat fine to the list. Adrenaline congregated in David's toes, sending them tapping in wild impatience. He didn't want to look at Candy until he was close enough to intervene, didn't want to think about how many dollars of cookies she'd have wolfed by now. With one eye on the traffic lights, David cast his other eye down to avoid the temptation of peeking at her. What he saw nearly made him jump out of his high-tops. At the base of the pier was a vast concrete toe, and it was tapping!

"Shit!" He stepped back, the cookie crisis forgotten. Of course it wasn't a living toe, it was just some kind of public art thing, but—
Ka-chunk, ka-chunk, ka-ka-ka-boom.

A deafening knot of traffic thundered overhead. David looked up in alarm when he heard an even stranger noise that sounded like "Ouch-ouch-ouch-gheez-oh-shit!"

He blinked his eyes, wiped his lenses and stepped back from the pier, looking up at the car-burdened decks of the Viaduct. Someone had sculpted barely discernable eyes in the side of the top deck. Some kind of public art thing, for sure, maybe with a recorded vocal track somewhere?

"Please, kid, please!"

There was no mouth, at least that he could see. Well, maybe just the hint of one.

And it moved.

"You gotta help me, kid!"

For once, David wished he was back in Utah.

Knuckles rapped crisply halfway up the penthouse door, breaking into Veronica's monologue of frustration about her unnamed dad.

"I'm terribly sorry," Jim said. He pushed the box of tissues towards her before he left his office. "Hold that thought. This shouldn't take a minute."

Someone five-foot-six, tops, Jim surmised as he squinted through the front door peek-hole at a riot of curly black hair. The espresso cart kid. On top of everything else, something was definitely wrong with the security spell on the building! Jim gritted his teeth and sighed. One hand reached for his wallet as the other reached for the doorknob. He steeled himself for the reparation the kid would demand after Candy's unfunded raid of the chocolate cookies. He'd seen it all from the office window when he'd seated Veronica for her counseling session.

"I'm really sorry about all this—"

The kid's eyes were wild and he cut Jim off before he could finish. "How do you talk to a giant?"

"Now really, young man, I know my wife is a bit on the Amazonian side—"

"Huh?"

"By Zeus, they make you mortals dense these days," he blurted. "I'm talking about the cookies. How much do I owe you for the cookies?" Jim thumbed through his billfold. "I have a couple of twenties—"

The kid's hands landed on top of his and pushed the wallet down.

"I'm not talking about the cookies, man. Ralph sent me."

Jim's oversized heart fell to his tube socks. "Now listen here," he stalled, scrambling to stay with the situation, trying not to imagine what Zeus would think was suitable punishment for revealing his powers to a mortal hatchling. He raised his wallet again. "I think forty dollars is more than fair for a purse full of cookies—"

The kid again shoved Jim's wallet out of the conversation.

"You're wasting time, Jim! That's your name, right? Ralph is going to do something really, really bad, really, really soon, if you don't talk him down!"

"Oh. I see. Is that all?"

Jim's knees sagged as if a baseball bat had hit them from behind. He steadied himself by flattening one palm on the door frame. That big concrete oaf had blabbed to a mortal! Served him right for not going to see Ralph for two days straight when he was in one of his moods. If things didn't improve fast, he could kiss even this miserable job goodbye.

"This is a bit of a shock. Excuse me—David, is it?" The kid nodded. "Where are my manners? Come in, sit down, we'll—we'll get it worked out." *I hope.*

Jim heard Veronica sniffling behind the office door as he showed David to a small-g-sized chair opposite the sofa. David perched on the edge of the seat, his feet dangling.

"Okay," said Jim, hunching forward from the sofa to make his face level with David's. "Tell me."

When Jim heard about Ralph's big toe, something inside of him snapped. He sprang to his feet and paced to the living room window that overlooked Ralph and Elliott Bay. The sun glinted off hundreds of cars charging over the top deck of the Viaduct. Jim made a fist and shook it hard.

"What are you trying to do, Ralph, ruin me?!"

"Hey."

Jim felt a small hand shake his elbow.

"Get it together, man. I know it sucks." David was staring at him, hard. "We've got to save those people, Jim!"

"We've got to save those people," Jim repeated, stunned. Working with a mortal, using his powers in front of a mortal witness—

both breaches were punishable by decertification. If Zeus heard about this, he'd be scrubbing pots in the kitchen at Athens Tech for the rest of eternity. But if mortal lives were on the line—

They both jumped when the front door crashed open.

"Better leave now," Jim decided instantly. He knelt before the window as he waved his hand to cast a glass removal spell. "Let's go, David. Wrap your arms around my neck."

"We're—we're flying?"

"I'm flying, you're riding. No time to discuss it, just hold on. Not too tight, though," Jim added, "especially by the jugular."

Arms circled neck and Jim shot neatly through the window as Candy stormed into the living room.

"Jim!" he heard her yell at the soles of his Doc Martens. "Come back here, you bastard! It's my birthday! It's my damned birthday, you creep!"

~ * ~

Veronica had overheard the entire conversation from inside Jim's office. First Dad had shown up and now this! Seattle would crash down around her ears, and not just figuratively, if something didn't happen fast.

Her therapeutically released tears forgotten, she paced like a caged tiger, arms crossed and muttering to herself. This was worse than one of those irritating case studies the Business Management professor liked to trot out once a semester at Athens U, the type where your score included identifying "need to know" information to resolve the study. How was it possible the espresso cart kid could hear and understand Ralph, could see his eyes and mouth etched in the Alaskan Way Viaduct, could get past the security spell that protected the Parthenon Building? The kid's glasses were as thick as the Minotaur's neck and besides, he was mortal!

Veronica came to a dead halt in the center of the office floor. Or was he?

The sound of breaking glass shrieked from the kitchen. Veronica rushed out to investigate. She found Candy rifling through a cupboard, tossing whatever was in her way to the floor.

"Where's that box of Dilettante truffles?" Candy's voice echoed from the back of the cupboard. "Fricking Jim and his midnight snacking!"

Veronica backed away on tip-toes but Candy spun around and

saw her.

"And what in the River Styx are you doing in here, you little bitch!?"

Veronica had never seen pupils so large. The woman was nuts, crazed, psycho!

"Wrapping up the audit," Veronica said, struggling to sound calm. Even being a Big-G didn't seem like enough to cross Candy and survive.

Candy's mouth formed a false, nasty smile. "Then we'll be seeing your sorry ass out the door soon? Good!" The small-g snorted and leaned back, her almost-too-big rear resting against the counter. "I've got half a mind to report you to the—" Candy glanced down, pretending, it seemed, to study her nails. She abruptly stared at the floor, her red-painted lips rounding in shock.

"My commemorative wine glass from Chateau St. Michelle!" she howled, bending to pick up a large, rounded shard decorated with gold etching. "Shit!" she continued to herself, "this was from our anniversary, the nice one, when Jim didn't get paged the whole weekend."

"Oh, for Dad's sake," Veronica muttered under her breath. Ralph was on the verge of destroying the Alaskan Way Viaduct and this fruitcake was crying over a broken glass! She waved her hand in a simple mending spell.

As the shards rose from the tile floor and re-formed to stemware in Candy's hand the small-g goddess jumped, nearly sending the glass to the floor again.

"How—?" her head spun toward Veronica. "Oh no," said Candy, setting the intact wineglass on the counter with a shaking hand. She squinted at the area just above Veronica's head. "Don't tell me you're a—"

"Straight from Mount Olympus."

Candy sagged and held her head in her hands. "Shit, shit, shit!"

"There's no time for that, Candy," Veronica snapped. "We're in the middle of a crisis!"

Candy looked up, mascara running. She tucked a wild gold tress behind her ear and sniffled.

"It's—it's my birthday. My four-thousandth birthday."

"If there's still a Seattle by sunset I'll buy you a cake. Now pull yourself together! If we don't figure out Ralph's problem fast, he and several thousand mortals will be history before lunch rush."

Veronica grabbed Candy by the wrist and dragged her to the glassless living room window. She waved her free hand, veiling them both with an invisibility cloak.

"On the count of three," she ordered.

They rose together, Candy's pulse hammering in Veronica's grip. She felt a jittery jolt starting in her palm and zapping through her body. Was it possible she'd picked up a chocolate contact high?

~ * ~

Even with David on his back the flight down Madison took mere seconds. Jim's brain was loaded to bursting with crisis and riddles. When they landed at the base of Ralph's piers, he felt like he'd been thinking way too hard, 24/7, for a thousand years. Not to mention the ethical dilemma. But he had no choice. He had to tell Ralph the truth about Cliffie.

Jim scripted the conversation in his mind, trying to dismiss the alarming fact David had the ability to talk to structurelings. He had a healthy, pink, mortal aura, nothing more. Was Seattle on the brink of an apocalypse?

He squatted upon landing. The instant he sensed David's feet touching the pavement he turned himself into a pigeon. White sun beat down on his feathers. By Zeus, it was hot this morning! He could barely flap up to perch on the concrete railing and look down into Ralph's eye molecules, which had condensed considerably into recognizable eyes since their last session.

"Hi, Ralph," he cooed.

"Jim! You gotta get me out of here!"

The Viaduct trembled under Jim's talons.

"Hold on, Ralph." Jim silently prayed to Zeus he could contain this crisis with words alone. "You've got to be brave a little bit longer."

"How long, Jim?" Ralph moaned. "Until they're driving two hundred thousand cars over me every day? I can't take it, I tell you. I'm cracking up!"

Ka-chunk, ka-chunk, ka-ka-ka-boom.

Jim could just make out nostrils flaring in the concrete.

"Ralph, think of the thousands of people who'll die if the Viaduct collapses!"

"I don't care anymore, Jim!" the structureling wailed. Rebar twisted in depths of concrete.

"Ralph," Jim screeched above the din. "You'll die without a Big-G to help you reconstitute!"

"I doesn't matter anymore, Jim. Nothing matters anymore."

A crowd had gathered below. A huge chunk of concrete cracked in the railing, showering the onlookers with a cloud of gritty dust. All but David scrambled for cover. Every car on the raised highway stopped. Some of the drivers and passengers abandoned their vehicles and stampeded down the lanes to the nearest exit.

Jim's intestines twisted in an unprecedented knot of anguish. A truth he'd pieced together decades ago but had held secret for reasons of confidentiality was the only tool he had left.

"Ralph, you've got to live!" he screeched. He hopped from the Viaduct and flapped furiously in front of Ralph's nearly restructured face. "You've got to live for your son!"

"Son?"

The heaving and cracking of concrete stopped, but the abrupt halt in motion sent the cracked hunk of railing crashing to the street.

"Goodbyyyyye, Jim!"

As Ralph's parting wail rang in Jim's ears a warm, strong wind rushed past him and sent him spiraling to the pavement. Jim's world went black.

David rushed over to Jim, sprawled flat on his back on the street, transformed to his true shape except for a few feathers that clung to his hands. He knelt beside the alien or god or whatever he was and yelled, "Wake up, man!" over the howl of the wind that had blown the pigeon Jim to the ground. He didn't dare lift Jim's shoulders and shake him in case his spine was injured. "Wake up, Jim," he pleaded. "It's not safe here, we gotta go!"

The wind stopped as suddenly as it had started. David looked up. The wail of sirens filled the air. A fire truck was deploying a ladder to the lower level of the Viaduct. Surveying the street, he glimpsed an extremely tall, sturdy man wearing a shabby gray toga. The man, shaggy with long gray hair and flowing beard, took huge, limping strides in their direction. He knelt on the other side of Jim. A vast tear splashed down his cheek.

"Do you think he's hurt bad?" The giant asked timidly.

As they looked down, Jim's eyelids fluttered. He peered through slits at David, then at the giant.

"Ralph? How come you're not dead?" Jim murmured, his voice hoarse and weak. His eyes closed again.

"He needs help," David said to the man who used to be a Viaduct. "Where on earth do you guys go for medical attention?"

They arrived in time to prevent complete and utter disaster. Veronica dropped Candy (none too gently) on the pavement and sprinted toward the heaving Viaduct. Ralph, though his molecules were dispersed just enough to keep the structure from crumbling to the ground, was visible in outline from the shoulders up. His face twisted in pain, grew more defined each second, then froze as he uttered, "Son?" Veronica launched upward and spoke the words of reconstitution as she flew past his right ear. Her own molecules disbursed in a warm rush and sank into quaking concrete.

It was the same sensation as diving into a pool, only Veronica, herself, was the water, not the diver. She'd never felt so fragmented in her life, not even during finals week at Athens U when she'd stay up all night cramming for exams. The transformation had been instant. She felt lucky it had worked at all, as until this moment she'd only known the theory. Her lung molecules, disparate as they were, sighed in collective relief when she spotted Ralph's humanoid form. Outlined by his small-g aura, he limped across the pavement below. The word "son" echoed in her consciousness. A series of thoughts tried to connect but the meaning floated just beyond her grasp.

The commuters were still running around screaming on the highway decks, bouncing her spine molecules into pulp. Her vision was diffuse, panoramic but fuzzy. She could clearly see heat and auras, even off the mortals. By Dad, how did the structurelings stand this existence? As soon as she got out of here she'd do everything she could to—

Logic hit a marble wall. She'd transformed in a moment of crisis without a comprehensive plan: only another Big-G God had the power to get her out!

"Tight spot, isn't it, Ronnie?" said a telekinetic voice.

Her eye molecules rolled toward the street. The aura was purple and gold and it emanated from the one being she simultaneously most and least wanted to see.

"You said it, Dad."

Another Big-G aura pulsed alongside him. A new voice sounded in her brain.

"Ronnie? Honey? Are you all right?"

Veronica's brow molecules furrowed. "Mom? What are you doing here?" she thought back.

"We'll talk about it later, sweetie," Hera said.

"We saw it all happen, Ronnie," Zeus said. "I'll have to admit, I'm impressed. It looks like they've taught you *something* practical at Athens U, though I can't say I agree with your career choice."

Even with fuzzy hearing she could detect the pride in Dad's voice.

"Thought I'd find out how the other folks live," she thought loudly, her ear molecules challenged by incoming aid car sirens. "You wouldn't like to try it yourself, would you?"

"I might be a little rusty at that stuff," Zeus said, his tone skeptical. "It's been millennia since the last time—"

"I'm looking for volunteers," her eye molecules shifted toward Hera, "and I see two."

"You think it would take both your mother and I to do what you can do?"

Great, now he was getting defensive, just like every other time she'd tried to sell him one of her ideas.

"Mom can fill in for Clifford," she said, ignoring the reprimand. "I need to get out of here, and I need Clifford to help me demonstrate the new structureling technology."

"If this is about that computer boar-wash again—"

Mom cut him off. "For your sake, Zeus, would you listen to her for once? Why are we putting her through college if you're not going to let her help you out of this mess?"

Black clouds rolled across the sky and thunder boomed on Puget Sound.

"I'd rather hold up the Alaskan Way Viaduct than listen to insults," Zeus fumed. "Stand by, Ronnie, I'll get you out."

Later she'd describe the sensation as being sucked into a vacuum canister. Her ears crackled with implosion and she staggered when her feet hit the pavement. Familiar hands grabbed her by the shoulders.

"Steady, Ronnie," Mom coached. "Let's get your land legs back."

When her vision cleared, Veronica saw a cluster of purple auras just past the pavement. Ralph rose from his knees, a long, limp form cradled in his arms. Giant tears splashed on the figure's XXL plaid shirt. A purple aura—with the faintest tinge of gold—hovered above the injured man. In a sickening instant, she recognized Jim. Candy, standing nearby, shivered and cried in silence. Mascara-blackened tears gushed down her cheeks as she took Jim's face in her hands and tenderly kissed his forehead. Unnoticed in the chaos of ambulances, fire trucks and news helicopters, the trio made a slow procession up the hill.

David sagged against a brick wall, looking stunned. He stood straighter when Veronica approached and vaguely glanced at Mom, whom, Veronica had just noticed, was dressed like a bag lady. His face was tear-streaked. "He's still got a pulse," David said with effort.

Veronica nodded to him and turned to Mom. "You saw his aura?"

Hera crossed her arms and pursed her lips. "Your father has some explaining to do."

"He could be Uncle Poseidon's, or maybe Uncle Hades'? He must have gotten that height from somewhere," she added.

Mom's stony stare said she was not convinced.

"Jim's part Big-G, Mom. Someone must have cloaked his aura when he was a baby. You know we're the only ones here who can heal him."

"So heal him, what do I care?" Hera snapped.

Veronica ignored the barb and took Mom's hand, turning her toward David.

"Mom, this is my friend David Bernstein," she said, placing Hera's hand in David's. "David, this is my mom, Hera." She clasped her hands over theirs, noticing Mom's expression had softened. Maybe she was coming to her senses?

"David, please take Mom to Jim and Candy's penthouse. She'll know what to do. And as soon as you can, I want both of you to meet me at the Space Needle."

~ ✳ ~

David stood alongside Hera and watched Veronica rise a few inches off the pavement before she turned invisible. He had the oddest sensation, like he could feel her moving through the air. When the sensation dissipated, he turned toward the sixtyish woman in bag lady garb.

"Do you mind if we walk to the penthouse instead of flying?" he said. "I'm feeling kinda queasy."

Hera took his arm without it being offered. Her grip was firm, her smile eerily bright. "That would be lovely. We can learn a little more about each other on the way."

"I'm new to all this," David said, amazed he didn't stammer. "I met Veronica Tuesday morning at the espresso cart, but I didn't know about all of this." He looked around to see if anyone was listening. Everyone nearby was preoccupied with the chaos on and around the Viaduct. "I mean, all this Olympus stuff Ralph told me about when he was—" he tilted his head toward the concrete structure that was now still and somehow looked stable, "—in there."

"It's pretty simple, once you learn the basics," Hera replied breezily. "Just like any other world-wide family business, with a few variations."

"Yeah, like you can disperse your molecules and disappear and fly."

"Minor details, truly."

They started up the hill to Third Avenue, Hera's stride as hearty as a girl's.

David's overwrought brain scrambled to recollect anything at all about Greek mythology. Hera, he was pretty sure, was the jealous wife of Zeus and the archetype of a shrew. Possibly there was something about her turning a woman Zeus had seduced into a tree? He resolved to stay on Hera's good side.

"So you're *the* Hera, right? I know it's stupid of me to ask, but...."

"I look more the part in my usual clothes," she said, chuckling. They looked both ways before crossing First Avenue, the traffic lights flashing in emergency mode. "What I want to know is, are you Thelma Bernstein's boy?"

"What?!"

She tugged him toward the sidewalk from the middle of the street where he'd stopped, stunned. "Thelma Bernstein of Salt Lake City, Utah?" she clarified as they began the ascent to Second.

David's chest constricted, harkening back to asthma attacks he'd suffered in childhood. "How do you know Mom?" he gasped.

"She worked for me centuries ago."

"Mom's forty-eight," he retorted.

"More like four thousand eight hundred," Hera said. "Oh dear." She slid her fingers down to his wrist and felt his pulse, "I hope this isn't too much for you. That's the danger of keeping a secret for a couple of millennia, I suppose."

"Are you saying Mom is—Mom is one of you?"

"Technically Thelma's a small-g god with limited powers, but yes, you could say she's one of us. So is Milton Bernstein."

"No way!" David cried, pulling out of her grip. "Dad's an accountant, not a god!"

"They've lived under cover for over two millennia," she said, then stopped and placed her hands—strong hands—on his shoulders. "Cover arranged for your safety."

"*My* safety?" David's blood chilled in his veins. "Lady, I don't care if you are Hera, you're crazy! I'm a Jewish kid from Salt Lake City!"

"Maybe not so crazy," she replied, looking deep into his eyes. "Who would look for one of my children there?"

David wobbled on the steeply angled sidewalk, as dazed as if he'd been hit over the head with a two-by-four.

"Come on," she said, tugging him uphill. "We'll talk about this later, after I've had a look at your friend Jim."

David's tongue felt thick in his mouth. After they'd crossed Second Avenue he'd regained enough motor control to say, "So I'm Veronica's brother?"

"Half-brother."

"You're—you're my mom?"

"Yes," she said, sounding the slightest bit exasperated.

The archetypal jealous wife had cheated on her husband? David wasn't sure he wanted to know the answer, but he couldn't stop the question, "Then who's my dad?"

"Later. I will tell you he's the one who insisted you be raised Jewish. Whew, what a hill," she said, briskly changing the subject as they rounded the corner on Third and neared the main entrance to Jim and Candy's building. "I hope they have an elevator."

They entered the penthouse, the front door ajar and sagging, and walked in gloomy silence to the master bedroom. Jim lay in the middle of a vast, round bed. He was covered to the neck with a red velvet comforter, his face so pale it made David think of viewing a corpse. Candy sat alongside Jim. She held his hand and cooed nonsense words, or maybe it was Greek? Ralph was there, too, standing on the other side of the bed like a stone sentinel, hands clasped behind his back, his expression grave.

Hera chose her position at the foot of the bed and looked at Jim as if she saw something no one else could see. She raised her hands, palms flattened and fingers spread, and closed her eyes, breathing deeply. Candy stopped her prattle. Ralph locked his eyes on Hera, who trembled slightly, dropped her hands and opened her eyes.

"Is there anything you can do for him?" the giant asked.

"It's a little early to tell," Hera said, looking soberly at Candy. "I need to make some repairs before I can form a prognosis."

Candy's eyes were fixed on Hera's. Though no words were spoken, a sheepish look bloomed across the younger woman's face.

Hera turned to the giant. "Ralph, I want you and David to go to Seattle Center and find Ronnie. She'll be waiting for you at the Space Needle. Tell her I'll fly there as soon as I can."

A weighty hand on David's shoulder turned him away from the bed and out the door.

"C'mon, kid," Ralph said, shepherding David to the elevator.

As the stainless steel doors closed in front of them David heard a vast tear splash on the elevator floor.

~ ✶ ~

As they rambled down Third Avenue the kid approached a man loitering near a bus stop who held a placard reading "No Job, No Home" and talked him out of four grimy bills. "For our fare," David explained to Ralph as they continued on their way. They shortly arrived at an open section of downtown Seattle paved with bricks and dotted with sculptures. David led the way to a metal door on the ground level of a multi-floor building. He paused to point up at concrete tracks before entering and climbing an echoing flight of stairs. At the top landing a door opened to bright daylight. Ralph followed David through a turnstile after the kid shoved the bills under the half-window in a metal kiosk and said, "For two. One way."

It was Ralph's first experience riding the Monorail as it had been constructed for the 1962 World's Fair, several years after he'd been dispersed into the Alaskan Way Viaduct. He followed David into the sleek tube and settled on a padded bench alongside him, feeling self-conscious when his weight depressed their side of the car at an angle like a slightly heeling sailing ship. The raised train lurched away from the platform. Ralph's thoughts returned to Jim as he'd last seen him, pale and still. He shook his shaggy head and squeezed his eyes tight for a moment.

"I sure hope Hera can fix him."

"We'll hope for the best, Ralph," David said, patting Ralph's shoulder.

Faint music chimed on David's person. The kid reached into his shorts pocket for the talking device all the mortals had these days. He flipped the device open and looked at the screen.

"Mom?"

The kid raised the device to his ear. His face looked pinched. The Monorail slowed to a stop. The conductor announced a slight delay due to routine systems testing.

Ralph stared out the window at the tree tops and the city streets, mesmerized by the change of view. Cars and people swarmed in the last minutes of Friday morning rush. No matter what happened, Ralph vowed he'd never again be dispersed into a raised highway. Confined in the stilled, stream-lined coach, his brow dampened with claustrophobic sweat.

"Hah!" the kid barked. "You dropped it in a toilet?" Ralph grew absorbed in David's lively but serious facial expressions as he listened some more, nodding. "Yeah, I've had a pretty strange week, too." For a moment it looked like he was going to say something more, but when the train lurched forward he said, "Gotta to, Mom. There's something I have to talk to you about, but I'm in the middle of something I can't get away from right now." His brow furrowed. "Yeah, when I get off work," he agreed, and, after a brief pause, "Love you too, Mom."

David pushed a button to end the conversation, shaking his head but only for a second because the device chimed again. When the kid looked down at the screen this time he heaved a huge sigh.

"Yes?"

The voice of the caller, which sounded like a man's voice to Ralph, railed without pause as David nodded his head and said "uh-huh" every few seconds. The Monorail slowed and the conductor announced their arrival at Seattle Center. The kid switched off the device, his face drawn.

"That was my boss," David said. "I mean my ex-boss. I just got fired and he said I can forget about my paycheck." The kid hung his head. "Dad will kill me." After a pause he added, "Whoever he is."

Dad. The word that he'd never taken personally suddenly filled Ralph with awe. Jim had told him he had a son!

Overwhelmed with emotion, Ralph's head sagged forward, his bearded chin touching his chest. On his first day of freedom, after a half-century and more dispersed in tons upon tons of steel and concrete, he'd learned he was a father!

The monorail halted at a concrete terminal.

"C'mon big guy," David said. His puny fist nudged Ralph's shoulder. "Time to see Veronica."

Little Ronnie! He would have died if she hadn't been there to reconstitute his molecules and take his place in the Viaduct. Wreathed with humility, Ralph rose from his seat and lumbered behind David, returning the conductor's curious glance as they debarked at Seattle Center. Every muscle in his body was stiff. As soon as he knew Jim was going to be okay Ralph vowed to take a long walk, his first since 1953, to get his body broken back in again.

To their left three huge metal legs curved skyward, grounded by a vast ground-level gift shop that encircled the base of the Space Needle. It had been bad enough, seeing the top third of the rival structure from his old spot in the Alaskan Way Viaduct, but the jealousy Ralph felt when he realized Cliffie commanded a brisk souvenir trade....

"Damn," Ralph muttered to himself. A series of taunts for the little wimp formed on his tongue but as they drew near the structure he saw something that drove the verbal barbs from his mind.

"Wow," said the kid as they halted side-by-side. The mortal visitors of Seattle Center were frozen in place, suspended in mid-stride like statues. All except for a tall, elegant woman with flowing white hair, dressed in a billowing red gown. The woman (Ralph realized it was Hera after noticing the purple and gold aura) stood in front of Cliffie with her arms raised, palms to the sky. Before his eyes she dissolved into glistening red particles, soared toward the observation deck at the top of the Space Needle, permeated the surface and disappeared.

A mild rumble shook the pavement beneath his sandaled feet. For the first time he noticed little Ronnie standing at the base of the structure, near the elevator doors. She was shaking hands with a tall young man. The fellow, lean with a cleft chin and dressed in a tweed jacket and flannel trousers, reminded him of someone from long ago. From his purple aura, the man was a small-g. He beamed a smile Ralph recognized when Veronica took his arm and led him forward.

"Ralph, there's someone I'd like you to meet. You too, David," she said, without taking her dark, dancing eyes from Ralph. "Ralph, this is your son, Clifford."

"My—?"

Swamped by a warm surge of emotion, Ralph couldn't say another word.

"I'm honored to meet you, sir," Clifford said, extending his large, square hand, but for the manicure a copy of Ralph's own.

Ralph bypassed the handshake and threw his arms around his son—his son!—in an embrace that would have crushed anyone but his own, dear boy.

Veronica observed David staring slack-jawed at the reunited giants. She tapped him on the shoulder. "Come on, let's give them some privacy." She led him to a nearby bench. He looked up toward the top of the Space Needle.

"Was that Hera in the red dress who—did whatever you call it to get Cliffie out?"

"Clifford." she corrected. "Yes, that was Mom. Red's a great color on her, don't you think? She borrowed a dress from Candy, she was so sick of her bag lady get-up."

David's head snapped toward her, his brow creasing. "Is Jim...?"

"He's going to be okay. Mom mended some broken ribs and repaired a few jostled organs before she flew over here. She says all he needs now is bed rest."

"Thank God. I mean," David rolled his eyes, "whomever."

"I've been telling Dad for two centuries, these structureling assignments are an accident waiting to happen," she said, partly to change the topic but mainly because the new technology Clifford had invented was so exciting she had to tell somebody about it. "There's a new approach to the job that I plan to implement as soon as Dad gives his authorization." Which shouldn't take long, as Zeus was stuck in the Alaskan Way Viaduct until he did as she asked. "It will take serious retraining effort, of course, and some staffing reassignments."

David gave her the oddest look, as if he was trying to make up his mind about something.

"Are you looking for new hires?" he finally asked.

She studied his dark, earnest eyes that (she'd learned from Hera's quick explanation minutes ago) came from Mom. It was a lot to absorb. Veronica tried her best to look upon David with compassion instead of shock and mostly succeeded. His cheeks had noticeably hollowed since she'd first met him on Tuesday, made him look vulnerable and younger than his two thousand years.

"Let's talk about it over breakfast," she said. Veronica waved a hand to release the mortals from their stasis and grabbed David's elbow. She tugged him to his feet and led him through a collection of groaning, elderly carnival rides to a multi-floor concrete building with brick façade and a colorful metal and neon awning. "Come on, little brother, you can show me what's good at the Center House."

They entered the hulking but reasonably engineered structure. The round clock mounted on the second level balcony read nine forty-five. Veronica's eyes flitted from booth to booth, zeroing in on the one vendor besides Starbucks (an option David refused for what he called "professional reasons") who had unlocked and rolled up the security gate in front of his concession. Doughnuts, eight varieties, and after shooting her an apologetic glance David ordered one of each. She ordered herself a drip coffee and they settled at a square table with two metal chairs. Veronica sipped the disgusting brew as her half-brother demolished his pile of sugar and grease. Just before starting the seventh doughnut he paused and mentioned he'd lost his job at the espresso stand. She slipped a few Euros across the tabletop, converting them to U. S. dollars before they reached his fingertips.

"Thanks," he said. "I owe you one."

"I'm staying at the Fairmont Olympic," she said, dreaming of the distant prospect of a deep night's sleep after a long soak and a bit of wine. "Call me in a couple of days and we'll talk about your future."

David's eyes widened at her last words. Doubtless it would take him some time to feel at ease with his new circumstances but she had more pressing business this morning; shepherding him through the ins and outs of immortality could wait. She said goodbye and headed back to the Space Needle.

The pieces of the Ralph, Briana and Clifford puzzle had come together during her flight from the Alaskan Way Viaduct to the Space Needle, aligned by her recollection that Jim had made the announcement Ralph had a son. Now the recently sprung structurelings needed some bonding time and a place to stay until they could find permanent living quarters. First she'd settle the two giants (who could be passed off as professional athletes if Ralph got some new clothes and a shave and they both got appropriate haircuts) into their own suites at the Fairmont Olympic. Next, she'd call Olympus, Inc., headquarters and tell them Zeus and Hera were temporarily on hiatus, and to direct all necessary business to her. She'd have to cover for Jim, too, supervising the other Seattle Area structurelings, but that could wait until Monday. She didn't want to leave Mom and Dad dispersed any longer than necessary. Tomorrow she'd meet with Clifford and start procurement for the test facility that would revolutionize structureling lives forever.

She hoped to Dad they'd succeed.

~ ✱ ~

Jim awoke in a darkened room, the hint of daylight glowing behind drawn shades. His vision was blurry. He drew his hand up to his face. The effort cost an unfathomable amount of energy. Confirming the absence of his glasses, Jim groaned. His hand dropped back alongside his body. He hadn't felt this bad since his chariot had lost a wheel and he'd been drug behind his team at an Athens U track and field meet a couple dozen centuries ago.

"Jim? Honey?"

A red blur crowned with a riot of gold stirred in the chair beside the bed.

His dry throat croaked, "Candy."

"Don't try to talk, sweetheart," she said in a gentle tone she hadn't used much in the last few centuries. Her hand, cool and soothing, stroked his brow. "You need complete bed rest, Jim. Hera says it's critical."

"Ralph. Is he…?"

"Ralph's fine, honey, everything's fine."

A thought, an important one lost in the disasters of the day, floated to the top of his memory.

"Birthday?"

"Yes, it's my birthday, Jim. And I got the best gift I could have hoped for." The red blur of her lips tilted upward. Perfect white teeth pierced the gloom. "You're going to be okay, Jim. Everything's going to be okay."

He blinked his eyes, overwhelmed by Candy's tenderness.

"Hera was great, Jim. She mended everything that was broken and ruptured—" Jim's eyes widened with shock, but Candy kept talking "—and she told me about some herbs to help with my PMS." She patted his hand. "You were right about that, honey, you were right all along."

Jim tried to roll to his side and sit up, but Candy gently eased him back on the bed and adjusted his pillows so he lay at a slight incline.

"Don't move a muscle, sweetheart, just tell me what you want and I'll get it for you."

A strand of her hair brushed his cheek, silk with the scent of rain.

"Behind the television," he said, too drained to speak a verb.

"Okay, honey, whatever you say," Candy replied, though her voice sounded doubtful.

She walked quietly to the next room. In moments, he heard a happy shriek.

"Oh Jim!" she said, rushing back to the bedroom, a brightly wrapped package clutched to her chest. "How sweet! You remembered my birthday after all!"

She resumed her chair and tore at the wrapping like an excited child.

"Oh!"

He couldn't see well enough to read the title with her, but the volume he'd reluctantly purchased last week was—

"*Doctor Apollo's Baby Book!* With a special foreword on natural childbirth by Ilithyia! Oh Jim!" He heard the crinkle of gift wrap falling to the floor. Candy knelt alongside the bed, took his hand and pressed it to her lips. "Oh Jim, honey, I'm so happy you want a baby too! We'll get started just as soon as you're well again."

He tried to tell Candy he had to call headquarters, had to let them know he'd be on sick leave and needed someone to fill in for him, but he was too exhausted to form the thoughts into words. The light behind the shades grew dim.

"I can start you on soft foods tomorrow," Candy said. "Hera wants you to get plenty of liquids until then." She touched a light kiss to his forehead, said she'd brew him a cup of herbal tea and left the room.

Alone, Jim pondered the happy reception of the baby book. He turned the word "father" over in his mind, contemplating its new, inescapably personal meaning. As he drifted back to sleep, he realized he was smiling.

ƏAY FIVE: SAƏURƏAY, ONE YEAR LATER

August in Seattle was temperate, for once.

Jim and Candy strolled the waterfront in the early afternoon, Candy's hand snuggled in the crook of Jim's arm while he propelled the pram, the wheeled barge of baby Titus. Jim squinted, peering half a block ahead. He raised an arm and waved.

"Hi, Ralph," he said as the giant's hulking form lumbered into focus.

"Hey, Jim. Hiya, Candy." Ralph's sense of fashion had evolved in the past year, a bright Hawaiian shirt, untucked, and XXL khaki shorts replacing his classic gray toga. "How ya doing, little guy?" he asked, bending over the baby buggy and wiggling his fingers near Titus' face. The baby cooed and wrapped a fist around Ralph's index finger.

Ralph chuckled. "This one's gonna be strong." He straightened to his full height, half a head taller than Jim, his eyes sparkling.

"He's finally sleeping through the night," Candy said, her smile tired and warm. "Maybe I'll be awake long enough to visit for a while when you come for dinner tonight."

"I still can't believe I have this kind of freedom," Ralph said. He shook his head and grinned. "When the new technology gets implemented in London I might even get to spend some time with Briana." The giant's chest rose with pride. "I still can't get over that boy of ours, he's quite a genius. Cliffie's really changed what it means to be a structureling."

"And a structureling counselor," Jim added, sighing with contentment as the August sun caressed his shoulders. Such a pleasant, relaxing day. He'd had lots of these since Veronica and Zeus had introduced the new organizational plan for the Olympus, Inc., former structureling division, now called "Architectural and Computer Sciences" or A & CS to insiders.

Six months ago they'd completed training for the transition. Cliffie (Jim heard Veronica's voice in his head, correcting the name to "Clifford") had been the driving force behind the plan of combining mortal computer technology with small-g structureling know-how. It was now possible for the small-g giants to perform their duties from a remote location instead of dispersing on site, and the technology offered an incredible new feature. Employees formerly known as structurelings (Jim and a focus group were working on a new name, appropriate to the new job description) could job-share because one worker could simultaneously monitor two structures, allowing for time off! Clifford and Ralph worked as a team, sharing the responsibility for the Alaskan Way Viaduct and the Space Needle. They split Monday-through-Friday into two twelve-hour shifts, with Ralph taking a break all day Saturday and Clifford doing likewise on Sunday.

"I love Jim's new schedule," Candy said. She gazed up at him and he warmed with pride. "Remember those crazy times when he'd be running off at all hours to talk you down, or listen to the Tacoma Dome's bitching? It seems like centuries ago!"

With the reorganized A & CS division Jim's job had changed, too, from Regional Supervisor and Counselor to Director of Architectural Support Personnel. He could set a regular schedule as the giants were now mobile and could call or come to his office for counseling and other appointments. This was all still in the beta-test phase, of course, but Veronica had confided in Jim her hope his role would become a global one, once the world-wide implementation of A & CS was complete. To date, Clifford had trained and monitored structureling teams throughout the Pacific Northwest. Aside from a personality conflict between Mavis of the Tacoma Dome (who knew it all) and old Henry of the Smith Tower (who resented Mavis' superior attitude), everything had gone smoothly.

Jim was gradually overcoming his discomfort in working as a team with two highly gifted individuals a generation younger than he. Sometimes he and Ralph got together over a beer and marveled at the brilliance and drive of Veronica and Clifford. Frankly, it made Jim feel old to work alongside them. But he and Ralph encouraged each other to keep heart and to keep moving forward, and Jim looked forward to the possibility of meaningful advancement for the first time in a long time. Veronica Zeta, Vice CEO of Olympus, Inc., had introduced profound changes to the structureling world, and to Jim's world along with it.

But the biggest transformation was in Candy. Jim slipped his arm from her grasp and wrapped it around her fit, tan shoulders to give her a squeeze. Whatever herbs Hera had recommended had leveled out her emotional spikes, and Candy was the Candy he'd known and loved before those last few awful centuries. She'd even stopped messing with the weather and was excited about Hera's offer to become part of the recently launched Marriage and the Media project. In a few more months, when she could take time away from Titus, Candy would start training part-time for television and radio talk show appearances. Jim held out great hope for her new career—in motherhood she looked more beautiful than ever, and her language had cleaned up dramatically since she first learned she was pregnant.

A gleeful cry rose from the pram and the rest of Jim's heart melted. Titus. What a dope he'd been, afraid to become a father! Overwhelmed with emotion, he barely noticed the young dark-haired man passing by who called out a greeting.

David had spotted the small-g group. At least that's how he thought of them. Jim, as it turned out, was half Big-G, one of Poseidon's offspring. Apparently the God of the Sea was as prolific as that old blues guy, Screamin' Jay Hawkins, when it came to fatherhood.

The question of David's own father had yet to be answered and Hera wasn't in a hurry to tell him. "I'll tell you when you're twenty-one hundred," she'd said, adding this was nearly a century away. The Bernsteins were relieved to have the truth known and at last be off the hook for David's safety and upbringing. David had flown down to see them—on his own power, no less!—for a couple of weeks after he'd lost his job with Use Your Bean. At first he'd vented a lot of frustration, feeling betrayed by their complicity in keeping Hera's secret. Thelma and Milton let him talk himself out and asked his forgiveness, and he did forgive them because they'd brought him up to be kind. Then they gave him back his history by removing a forgetfulness charm they'd renewed from time-to-time over the centuries. This proved an incredible gift as David could now remember, firsthand, bits and pieces of history—not just his own, but the world's—all the way back to when he was two hundred years old!

Thelma and Milton stayed on as his official parents of record, and Dad (David figured he would call him that until at least his twenty-first hundredth birthday) finally had a reason to take pride in him. David had returned to the University of Washington last winter and was making the dean's list, working toward a double major in computer sciences and architecture.

Going back to college was all part of Veronica's plan to work him into the role of liaison between mortal and immortal technological capabilities, someone "half-and-half" as she'd said the day he'd agreed to resume his studies. He'd never experienced the kind of demanding but constructive support his half-sister graced him with, the piece that was missing when he'd tried college before.

Hera (he couldn't bring himself to call her Mom) was a different matter. She'd been to Seattle once this year, to meet with Candy about the new Marriage and the Media project. She was friendly enough and had taken him out to dinner during her trip. After she'd worked through a half-carafe of wine he'd try to weasel his father's identity out of her, without success. He hoped she'd give in and tell him before 2110, when he'd turn twenty-one hundred. David wondered if he'd ever develop an immortal's patience, waiting for centuries to pass as if they were years.

But today was a perfect summer day and he didn't mind lingering in it. He'd caught the bus downtown from his U-District apartment to take a breather from a weekend of studying. Veronica had come to Seattle a couple of days early for a quarterly reorganization review with Jim and Clifford and she was meeting him for lunch. David scanned the crowded waterfront food court, searching for her. She waved to him from Ivar's Fish stand on Pier 56, looking festive and relaxed in a red mini-toga.

Though dressed casually and presenting David with a holiday façade, Veronica's mind was working overtime. Heaven and Earth be praised the Architectural and Computer Sciences department restructure was well underway. Even Dad had grudgingly admitted to the wisdom of this change after spending a few weeks holding up the Alaskan Way Viaduct.

But that was just the tip of the Olympus, Inc., iceberg. Her elder siblings, a hopeless and expensive tangle of misdirected corporate largess, were the next stop on the road to reform. All four of them performed their jobs haphazardly, emotionally and without a shred of self-discipline. Ares was the worst by far. Taking on this cowardly bully who delighted in war and destruction of mortals against mortals was Veronica's top priority. Even during her meeting-packed Seattle visit she was working on a plan for world peace, with the side-benefit of exiling Ares' sorry behind to the planet named after his Roman counter-part.

She concealed her concerns from David with a bright smile. "Happy study break," she said, handing him a tray loaded with two orders of halibut and chips with slaw on the side and huge waxed paper cups of lemonade. She led him through the tourist-filled outdoor dining area to a two-top near the waterfront railing—great view, and a negligible amount of seagull droppings on the table.

"My first final's Monday," David said. He slid onto the dark blue plastic seat opposite hers and grabbed one of two paper napkins bundled with plastic cutlery. "Got any plans for the weekend?"

"Lunch with you today and a matinee tomorrow. The Seattle Rep is doing something by Aristophanes."

"Going with anyone I know?" he said, wiggling his thick eyebrows in insinuation.

She blushed. "We're just friends, David. Clifford and I were raised by parents who took us to the theater." She and Clifford had talked with each other regularly for work reasons, and she enjoyed their conversations but rebuffed his efforts to get more involved. She simply didn't have time for that kind of relationship. Besides, Bill Gates, Jr., would never approve, as Clifford was allergic to cats.

She selected a fry from the top of the blue and white cardboard container and tossed it to a young seagull who hovered nearby in adolescent dark gray plumage. A wild chorus of screeching muted the constant rumble of traffic on the Alaskan Way Viaduct when adult gulls spotted the transaction. They spiraled around the table until Veronica repelled them with a look they understood.

"I'm glad you acted on my suggestion to matriculate year 'round," she said. "The sooner you finish your undergraduate work, the sooner you can start your master's degree at Athens U."

David downed a chunk of deep-fried halibut in two bites like any hungry young man. He'd filled out since last year. His face looked more solid, more like Mom's.

"Mom said to tell you hello," she said. David grunted, his mouth full. "She's really excited about The Marriage and the Media project, and Candy's makeover did her a world of good. Dad, too," she said with a grin.

David washed his food down with a gulp of lemonade. "How is your dad?"

Veronica didn't envy her half-brother being the only known fruit of Hera's adventures in cuckolding Zeus. Even semi-retired, the Lord of the Universe was no one to mess with. She raised her eyebrows, searching for informative yet neutral words.

"Pretty well, I think. I've had to adjust the re-organization timeline once already, after only a year," she said, wrinkling her nose. "Can you believe it? Most of the time he seems to be trying pretty hard to hand things over, but he has his pet projects. Giving up the structurelings is really hard for him. He invented that job, you know. What he was able to do with molecules was cutting edge at the time."

David made an assenting noise around a mouthful of fries. So much had happened for him in one year, since he'd haphazardly entered the world of the immortals, a world where flying and cloaking and, until recently, dispersing molecules were common work practices.

Veronica looked past David, across Alaskan Way at the Viaduct. He, too, half-turned toward the hulking gray mass across the street. A year had passed since the disastrous near-collapse, since David's half Big-G nature had overridden Thelma Bernstein's cloaking (which included disguising him with a pink mortal aura) just in time to save Ralph from crumbling to destruction. The only explanation anyone could think of was Thelma had been out of cell phone contact with David for several days and the cloaking had started to lose its charge, but no one, not even Clifford, had figured out the proof for this.

The Viaduct, with the help of the A & CS department, continued to support over one hundred thousand vehicles each day. It was still on the block for demolition and replacement with an underground tunnel, but city and state finances, hampered by a deep recession and a slow recovery, had pushed the project into the indefinite future. At her urging, David focused his term papers on some aspect of the Alaskan Way Viaduct and sometimes he'd e-mail her about the status of the proposed replacement structure, the complications with seawalls, the years-long interruption the new construction would cause. Maybe, just maybe, the mortal architects and engineers would build a truly self-sustaining structure this time?

David's hand waved in front of her face. "Hello? Earth to Veronica."

Veronica blinked and regarded him with a half-smile.

"Whatever you're thinking about, it'll keep, but your food's getting cold."

They both laughed and dug into the chips.

about the author

S. D. Matley writes novels and short stories. Her stories have been published by THEMA, GlassFire Magazine, Blade Red Press and The Absent Willow Review. Small-g City is her debut novella.

She lives in the Pacific Northwest with her husband, one dog, one horse and many pampered cats.

Get ready for more adventures with these fantasy books from WolfSinger Publications.

Call of Chaos – Carol Hightshoe

The exiled daughter of a minor noble, Kyrianna Dalynne, finds herself trapped in a temple dedicated to Thynitic, The Lady of Chaos.

She and her companions are charged with finding an ancient artifact before the ones guarding the portals out will allow them to leave.

As their search continues, Kyrianna begins to question if there was a specific reason she and the others were brought to this place.

The Twelve – James K Burk

Valtierra, a city-state, is governed by archetypes. Every two years they choose twelve men and women to wear the masks and to become the Wise Old Man, the Fool, the Mother, the Harlot, the Warrior, and the rest of the council. But now Valtierra faces hunger, decay, and an enemy on their border and, when the need for leadership is greatest, one mask is worn by a foreigner and one mask hides a traitor.

High Rage – James K Burk

Scarface, on his way back to a clan stronghold after assassinating a legate, meets and falls in love with a woman even more ruthless than he. To win her, he must reunite an empire and create a kingdom. His only allies are his wits, his sword, and the power in his scars—black marks like the taloned finger prints of a demon.

To achieve his goals, he must deal with old enemies, gods of dubious worth, and his own family—who may be the most dangerous of all.

Taking Hope – James K Burk

The power he once held depleted, Scarface has found contentment as Morgan. No longer seeking power or building kingdoms, he is happy with his current life and with his wife Topaz.

However, when what he most loves is threatened, Morgan must again become Scarface to correct past mistakes. He must defeat a king and a god. Knowing one god can only be beaten by another, he seeks an alliance, but what price will be demanded?

With only a few allies, one of them mad with rage, and the power in his scars returned, he must confront old enemies, including one who knows his deepest secret and greatest weakness. Will he be able to lay to rest his past, defeat his enemies and return to the life he has made for himself? Or will he lose everything and everyone he has come to truly care about?

The Road to the Golden Griffin Series – Jason J Sergi

The Dragon King and The Golden Griffin. It's an ancient story, created back when the world was still wild. A story of a wise but fierce ruler, and a bold usurper. A story of strange beings, and fabled treasure. A story with origins lost to legends, wars, and the taming of the world. A story that has attracted hundreds of adventurers and treasure hunters to the dangerous lands of the long-dead dragon king. A story that has intrigued young Bathmal Arined since the day he heard it and now that very story has sent him down a road which passes through cosmic strife, bitter loss, horrid evil, and uncertain friendships.

The road can only end with The Golden Griffin…
or Bathmal's death.

Book 1: The Hero of Twilight

Millstand held very little for young Bathmal Arined. Aside from his mother, the village held nothing for him at all. And yet, he was trapped within its confines. Born fantasizing of grand adventure and of places wholly unlike Millstand. Places where everyone had a voice, and everyone mattered and cared for one another regardless of caste.

He often spent long hours wandering the worlds of his imagination, battling evil singlehandedly, rescuing cities and nations from hordes of gruesome demons, and returning to countless glorious homecomings.

But when the fantasies faded and reality crept back in, Bathmal knew he was just a bastard; and in his world, that equaled to nothing. Then, on a cold winter day on the outskirts of the village, Bathmal's life changes forever. He encounters a knight from the north, who tells Bathmal that there is more to the world than being a bastard, and that even bastards can become knights. Bathmal becomes obsessed with the idea and follows the knight from the village and commences on a life journey that will take him into the frozen mountains, across the sea to an ill-fated kingdom, and into the depths of The Black Realm of Hadez itself, there to face his true tests where success would grant Bathmal the chance to obtain everything he'd dreamed of, and failure meant endless death.

Bathmal's journey also leads him to the tale of The Golden Griffin, and sets him down the first few steps of the road towards a possible meeting with history…and a legend come alive.

Book 2: The Threat of Saint Flesh

Bathmal, now a knight of a defunct Order, returns home to revel in his accomplishment, and to rescue his mother from the backbreaking misery offered by Millstand's fullbloods.

But upon returning, Bathmal and Nojo find Millstand deserted and ransacked, his mother and everyone else gone. There is little evidence as to what had happened to the townfolk, but of what evidence there is, it all pointed north. Together, Bathmal and his consquire charge north through Anfaria's badlands in a desperate attempt to find answers. Along the way they unravel a hideous plot that must be stopped before it can go any further. They also find an old friend of Sir Odon's, whose loyalty is suspect; and a demon far worse than anything Bathmal has ever faced before.

Bathmal needs to find his mother if at all possible, but his duty as a knight may suck him too deeply into the cosmic battles being waged by Deus and Malus. And to compound all else, betrayal and a new war awaits him across the sea in Twilight—but another danger, one which lies much closer, threatens to destroy him and all that he hopes to achieve…

Another detour along a Road where nothing is guaranteed. The Golden Griffin will wait…Bathmal needs only to survive.

Book 3: The Hunters of Shadow

The Battle of Delldoan is over; The Demon Saint Flesh is dead; the threat to Anfaria defeated; but, even with all this good fortune, Bathmal is left feeling lost and anxious.

His friend Sir Kasper is still among the missing long after The Battle of Delldoan has concluded, as is the vile dark-elf Zenlem Sidor. And, perhaps most troubling of all, Nojo-his trusted and faithful con-squire-continues to display signs of Dangerous Instability. If a solution to the problem cannot be found soon, Bathmal fears he may have to do the unthinkable…

Once more he will head into darkness, in hopes of finding Sir Kasper, and ridding the world of the dark-elf Sidor. But unseen forces will try to prevent him from doing both, and Bathmal will soon find out the taint of Hadez lasts far longer and doesn't go away just because he is no longer within the fell realm; but when the time comes, will he decide to fight against the taint, or will he embrace it?

The Golden Griffin waits for Bathmal…possibly forever…

Find out more about these and our other books at
www.wolfsingerpubs.com